IF I RUN

BOOKS BY TERRI BLACKSTOCK

THE MOONLIGHTERS SERIES
1 *Truth Stained Lies*
2 *Distortion*
3 *Twisted Innocence*

THE RESTORATION SERIES
1 *Last Light*
2 *Night Light*
3 *True Light*
4 *Dawn's Light*

THE INTERVENTION SERIES
1 *Intervention*
2 *Vicious Cycle*
3 *Downfall*

THE CAPE REFUGE SERIES
1 *Cape Refuge*
2 *Southern Storm*
3 *River's Edge*
4 *Breaker's Reef*

NEWPOINTE 911
1 *Private Justice*
2 *Shadow of Doubt*
3 *Word of Honor*
4 *Trial by Fire*
5 *Line of Duty*

THE SUN COAST CHRONICLES
1 *Evidence of Mercy*
2 *Justifiable Means*
3 *Ulterior Motives*
4 *Presumption of Guilt*

SECOND CHANCES
1 *Never Again Good-bye*
2 *When Dreams Cross*
3 *Blind Trust*
4 *Broken Wings*

WITH BEVERLY LAHAYE
1 *Seasons Under Heaven*
2 *Showers in Season*
3 *Times and Seasons*
4 *Season of Blessing*

NOVELLAS
Seaside
The Listener (formerly
The Heart Reader)
The Heart Reader of Franklin High
The Gifted
The Gifted Sophomores

OTHER BOOKS
Shadow in Serenity
Predator
Double Minds
*Soul Restoration: Hope
for the Weary*
Emerald Windows
Miracles (*The Listener / The Gifted*)
Covenant Child
Sweet Delights
Chance of Loving You

PRAISE FOR TERRI BLACKSTOCK

"Blackstock's newest novel, *If I Run*, is the best suspense novel I've read in decades. Boiling with secrets, nail-biting suspense, and exquisitely developed characters, it's a story that grabs hold and never lets go. Read this one. Run to get it! It's that good."

—Colleen Coble, *USA Today* bestselling author of
Mermaid Moon and the Hope Beach series

"The exciting and heart-pounding conclusion to Blackstock's Moonlighters trilogy is quite a thrill ride. The intrigue and danger come to a dramatic culmination as the villain gets backed into a corner."

—*Romantic Times* on *Twisted Innocence*

"Blackstock fans will be drawn to this third novel in the Moonlighters series with its themes of forgiveness and second chances. While being able to be read as standalone fiction, readers will enjoy a richer character understanding having read the previous books."

—*CBA Retailers + Resources* on *Twisted Innocence*

"The second book in Blackstock's Moonlighters series starts off with a frightening incident and is filled with action from that point forward. A multilayered story of deception, greed, and secrets unravels at a perfect pace to keep readers interested and entertained."

—*RT Book Reviews*, 4 star review of *Distortion*

"Blackstock has such a way with characters that they can get away with almost anything—like being part of a family with an unreasonably high body count—and still manage to be believable. *Distortion* is a good suspense novel but more than that it brings up a number of attitudes and actions that will have readers examining their own thought patterns and values."

—Crosswalk.com

"Crisp prose, an engaging story, and brisk pacing make this thriller another home run for Blackstock. Recommend it to readers who enjoy material by Lynette Eason and Erin Healy."

—*Library Journal*, starred review of *Downfall*

"A story rich with texture and suspense, this family murder mystery unfolds with fast pacing, a creepy clown murder suspect, and threatening blog visitor to boot."

—*Publishers Weekly* on *Truth Stained Lies*

"The Restoration series comes to a dramatic end. Blackstock is absolutely masterful at bringing spiritual dilemmas to the surface and allowing readers to wrestle with them alongside her characters. This is a fitting conclusion to this unique series."

—*RT Book Reviews*, 4¹/₂ star review of *Dawn's Light*

"Good writing, well-honed descriptive details, compelling characters, and a conclusion that doesn't succumb to pat answers keep the pages turning, making this an engaging novel for fans of Christian nail-biters."

—*Publishers Weekly* on *Cape Refuge*

"Blackstock's superior writing will keep readers turning pages late into the night to discover the identity of the culprit in this amazing mystery. The unique setting and peek into the Nashville music scene are fascinating. Suspense lovers are in for a delightful treat."

—*RT Book Reviews*, 4¹/₂ star review, TOP PICK! on *Double Minds*, 2009 Nomination for Best Inspirational Novel

"Drawn in from the first line, my heart ached for Kara, Lizzie, and their moving story. The satisfying end didn't stop the lingering sadness, as there's so much more to this novel than just the life of two little girls and the wounds that should never have been. Ms. Blackstock tactfully and skillfully deals with the undesirable traits of her characters (promiscuity and subsequent abortion, which are briefly mentioned). The book is so well written it is hard to believe it's just fiction!"

—*RT Book Reviews*, 4 star review of *Covenant Child*

"In a departure from her usual heart-stopping mysteries, Blackstock delves into the world of a con man who meets his match. This fast-paced novel doesn't provide any astounding twists, but the story is incredibly well told and will keep the reader fascinated until the last page."

—*RT Book Reviews*, 4 star review of *Shadow in Serenity*

IF I RUN

TERRI BLACKSTOCK

NEW YORK TIMES BESTSELLING AUTHOR

 **ZONDERVAN®**

ZONDERVAN

If I Run

Copyright © 2016 by Terri Blackstock

This title is also available as a Zondervan ebook.
Visit www.zondervan.com/ebooks.

This title is also available as a Zondervan audio book.
Visit www.zondervan.com/fm.

Requests for information should be addressed to:
Zondervan, 3900 Sparks Dr. SE, Grand Rapids, Michigan 49546

Library of Congress Cataloging-in-Publication Data

Blackstock, Terri, 1957-
If I run / Terri Blackstock.
  pages; cm
ISBN 978-0-310-33243-5 (paperback)
I. Title.
PS3552.L342851з 2016
813'.54--dc23
2015032139

ISBN 978-0-310-33244-2 (library edition)

Scripture quotations are taken from the New American Standard Bible®, Copyright
© 1960, 1962, 1963, 1968, 1971, 1972, 1973, 1975, 1977, 1995 by The Lockman
Foundation. Used by permission. (www.Lockman.org)

Published in association with the literary agency of Alive Communications,
Inc., 7680 Goddard Street, Suite 200, Colorado Springs, CO 80920, www.
alivecommunications.com.

Interior design: Lori Lynch

Printed in the United States of America

16 17 18 19 20 RRD 10 9 8 7 6 5 4 3 2 1

This book is lovingly dedicated to the Nazarene.

1

CASEY

There's blood on the bottom of my shoes. I rinse the soles, knowing the police will trace the impression of the rubber pattern and determine that they're Skechers. They'll find the charge for the shoe store on my credit card, proving they're mine.

Blood runs down the drain. My heart races as though it's my own draining away, but it's not mine. My throat constricts as tears fill my eyes, but I push them away. There's no time to feel.

When the shoes seem clean enough, I blot them on a towel and slip them into my bag.

They'll see the traces of blood on the sink, in the footsteps at the door where I took the shoes off, on the towel. They'll shine that luminol stuff all through my apartment and add it to the evidence list against me. There's no point in wasting time cleaning it up. I just have to get out of here.

It's not easy to pack your life into a duffel bag, but I have no other options. I pack what I think I'll need—a skirt, two pairs of jeans, some shirts, a pair of scissors for cutting my hair as soon as I'm in a safe place, underwear, mascara, toothpaste and toothbrush, contacts case and glasses. I go to my dresser and slide out the drawer, dig past my socks to the cigar box at the back. I open it. The stacks of hundred-dollar bills are still there. This is my rainy day, the emergency I need the cash for. I stuff the stacks into my bag's pockets, then hurry into my tiny living room/kitchen combo and grab the framed pictures of my family from a shelf. I stuff them into the bag too.

Quickly, I write a check for my rent, tear it out, and leave it on the counter with a note to the landlord that he can rent my apartment and donate what I've left to Goodwill. I don't want him left holding the bag. I think of calling work and telling them I won't be back in, but it's better if I don't.

I slip my purse strap over my shoulder and carry the duffel out, then lock my apartment behind me, though I don't know why.

I see the blood on my car door handle as I get in. Ignoring it, I drive to a parking garage at a hotel downtown, leave it without looking back, and ride the elevator down to the hotel's first floor. I slip into the ladies' room and pull my hair up in a ponytail, then tie a bandana around my head. I take out my contacts, wash off my eye makeup, and shove on my glasses. Then I carry my purse and duffel bag through the hotel's glass doors to the driveway, where cabs are waiting. I tip the bellman as he signals to one for me.

I get in and tell the driver to take me to the bus station.

They're probably not looking for me yet. It will be a while before they discover Brent's body. I give in to the temptation to pray, though I don't know if anyone will hear. I have trouble believing in God, but when I'm in a mess, my mind often formulates quiet pleas. I don't know what to ask for. Time? Distance? An escape path?

Justice?

Yeah, right.

I ask for help in general, trusting that if there's someone on the other end of those prayers, he'll know what I need. Loneliness falls over me like a fog as we drive through my town, and I wonder what I'll do without my friends. I love people. Always have. I don't like being alone.

And my family. My six-month-old niece who adds a new trick to her baby repertoire every week . . . will I ever see her again? The thought of never rocking her to sleep again is almost as brutal as the image of my best friend lying dead on the floor.

I let my eyes linger on the town I've grown to love. Funny, I didn't know I loved it until now.

I struggle to keep my mind from going back to what happened earlier. An hour ago? Two hours? I force my thoughts from the terror of it.

One step at a time. Get to the bus station. Then I can cry.

2

———

CASEY

I've never been to the bus station before. It holds a dirty mystique—a sense of unknown that I dread—but I know I can't use my car to get out of town. They will surely be looking for it. The airport is out of the question. Too many cameras and too much security. I hope I won't be immediately identifiable if my face suddenly flashes on the security screens from the cameras overhead. I look at the faded marquee with destinations and times flashing by. I have no idea where to go.

It has to be somewhere far enough away that my face won't appear on their local news. Somewhere that has no connection to me and no reason to draw me. Someplace I would never go.

And it needs to be one of the next buses out, wherever that will take me. I won't go all the way. I'll get off at one of the stops along the way.

But first things first. I find the women's restroom, glance under the stall doors to see if I'm alone. For now, I am. I stand in front of the dirty sinks and gaze into the mirror. Unzipping my bag, I pull out the scissors. I tug my blonde hair out of the bun, brush it out, and smooth my hand through it one last time.

My hair has always been my best asset, and I hate seeing it go. But I can't let vanity stop me. I scissor into it right at my jawline and watch the pieces of me fall to the floor. I don't slow down to dwell on it. I quickly hack my way around the back to the other side.

It looks like a home-cut bob, but it could be worse. It's still too much like me. I sweep it behind my ears—some change, but not enough. Should I cut it shorter in some kind of pixie look? No, that would take too long, and the amateur quality of the cut might draw more attention. This will have to do until I can get someplace where I can dye it.

I take a wad of cash out of my bag and shove it into my jeans pocket. I'll need to keep it close.

I squat and sweep up the discarded hair, take it to the toilet and flush it, then go back with a wet paper towel and wipe the floor, just to make sure no blonde dust is left there. I go back to the toilet and flush again, then stand for a moment watching the old Casey swirl around the bottom of the bowl before disappearing down the hole.

———

I lean back on the stall door. I can do this. I've endured hard things before. All I need to do is the thing police least expect. My life will depend on it.

I open my cell phone, remove the battery, and toss it into the trash. Then I break the phone and slip the pieces into my pocket to dispose of somewhere else along the way. I'm not sure whether it will work to keep police from locating me through the GPS on my phone, but I've seen criminals do it on TV shows.

I step out of the bathroom, glance around the terminal, and find a ticket window that doesn't have a line. My purse and duffel bag hanging from my shoulder, I step up to the clerk.

"Where to?" she says without looking up.

"Umm . . . what's the bus that's boarding right now?"

The woman looks up now. Our eyes meet, but I don't feel seen. "El Paso. Leaves in twenty minutes."

I don't take time to think. "Perfect. El Paso is the one I wanted."

The woman seems sleepy as she prints out the ticket and takes my money. "Better hurry."

I thank her and rush out to the bus. I let the driver scan my ticket, and he reaches for my bag.

"That's okay," I say. "I'll keep it with me."

"Might be a full bus. Nowhere to put it."

I had no idea El Paso was such a popular destination from Shreveport. "I'll stuff it under my feet. How long is this trip?"

"Ten and a half hours, give or take."

That's probably good. The longer I'm holed up on a bus,

the better. If they don't figure out how I got out of town, it could be a good place to be off the grid for a while.

I climb onto the bus. It's about half full so far. I walk down the aisle, avoiding the family with two preschoolers, and choose a window seat in an empty row. I drop my purse and bag into the seat next to me.

But soon the seats are filling up. I try not to make eye contact with those getting on looking for a seat. A man with a limp who barely made it up the steps, a teenaged kid with dark circles under his eyes and earbuds in his ears, an older woman with a cane, a soldier in fatigues carrying an army-issue bag.

The soldier checks me out and pauses at my seat. "Anybody sitting here?" he asks, pointing to my bag.

I don't like rejecting a soldier. We've asked so much of them, and they expect so little from us. I shake my head and move my bags to the space by my feet. He slips in, his broad shoulders brushing mine.

"Going to El Paso?" he asks.

"No, I'll be getting off along the way. Are you from El Paso?"

"Yeah," he says. "I've been gone for over a year. Afghanistan."

"They don't fly you home?" I ask, astonished.

"They flew me to where I deployed from, but that's not where my family is. I didn't want to go straight home," he says. "I wanted to stop off and visit a buddy's family. He didn't make it home, so . . ."

My heart swells. He must be a nice guy if he put his own homecoming second to the family of a dead friend.

"It's not that long on the bus."

"Who's waiting for you there?" I ask.

"My parents," he says. "And a girlfriend. I'm really anxious to see all of them."

"I bet they're dying to see you."

"Yeah, it's going to be a great weekend," he says, then swallows hard. "I'm a little nervous."

I get that. He's probably changed since leaving for war. Stepping back into a relationship will be awkward and difficult. My friend Nora's husband left on deployment four weeks after their first baby was born and was gone for a year. He did what little bonding he could do through Skype, but it wasn't the same. You just can't get back those months.

When he came home, Nora's joy quickly changed to silent concern, and we all knew things weren't going well. A person changes after a year as a mother . . . after a year as a warrior. Sometimes they change in opposite directions. I hope this soldier's girl treats him like a hero and gives him the time and space he'll need to adjust.

When he puts headphones on, I'm relieved that he doesn't want to know about me. I shove my own earbuds in, close my eyes, and pretend to sleep, but as the bus begins to roll away from the depot, I open them to see my town going by. I may never see it again.

I close my eyes again when tears spring to them. I can do this, I tell myself. I'm strong. I'm focused. I'm determined.

I won't let them win.

The tears abate. I wish I had actual music to drown out my thoughts, but my phone is broken in my pocket. Still, the earbuds keep me isolated.

I'm not sure if that's good or bad.

3

CASEY

When we stop at a Greyhound station in Dallas, I decide to get off and spend the night there. The bus will go on to El Paso, but I won't be on it.

There's an Overnight Inn in sight of the bus station, so I walk there, afraid I'll be mugged before I reach it. The night is alive with shadows and movement, but I walk briskly, my heart pounding. Halfway there, despair hits me like a sledgehammer across the temple. I can't believe I'm here, hiding from the law. My parents raised me to respect authority and believe in the system . . . but that was before the system turned on us.

To my family, committing murder is as foreign as committing suicide.

We aren't quitters, I told myself so many times after my father's death thirteen years ago. *He would never have hanged himself.* I was so sure of that when I found him, his body staged to look like someone who wanted to end it all. Even at twelve, I knew what I saw. My sweet dad dead in a way that he would never have wanted me to find him.

Now I wonder if I could be a real first in my family. Could I be the one who really does give up?

Maybe if I'm mugged and murdered, that would be the best thing. But my survival instinct is too keen, so I walk as fast as I can until I get to the front door of the hotel. They do have vacancies, so I tell them that my wallet was stolen but that I have cash. I register under a fake name and soon have my room key.

When I get into the room, it smells of mildew and cigarettes. The bed is hard and the sheet doesn't cover the mattress, but I tell myself I'm lucky to be here instead of jail.

Hopelessness sinks its claws deeper into me, and the thought of suicide returns. I think about how I might go about it, how I could cause the least trauma to whoever stumbles onto me. For a few minutes I rest in the thought that it could be over soon, in the relief it would be to not have to run for my life and hide like a criminal. I wouldn't have to worry about how to earn a living or where to live or who is closing in on me. I wouldn't have to deal with being branded a killer.

But I can't rest in that fantasy long. I think of my mom standing at a funeral visitation, repeating her OCD rituals ninety to nothing as she shakes hands and comforts the comforters. After the funeral, she will lie awake all night with terrors running through her head, not able to sleep for weeks until a doctor intervenes and adjusts her dosage. My sister will be so distraught and distracted that it will disrupt her parenting of little Emma. Her marriage will suffer because the bitterness and anger will rise like lava in her heart, and eventually she'll say something publicly that she shouldn't, and they'll come for her too.

They'll talk about my suicide on TV like I'm the drama of the week. They'll describe it in detail and there will be YouTube videos of my body. Nancy Grace will perform my psychological autopsy.

I finally bag the idea. Taking my own life would be too selfish. Too many dominoes would fall, too many people would be impacted, and not just for a day or a week or a month, but for years . . . for decades.

You can't just check out and think it will all be over. It won't be over for anyone who loves you. You'll only leave them to run after the pieces that scatter in the angry wind. You'll leave them desperately trying to solve the problems you wouldn't . . . all while plugging their own wounds. Even if you're like me, single without children, you could impact generations.

Is quick relief worth it?

No, it isn't. I'd rather take the pain myself so they won't have to.

There's no sense of relief when I determine that I have to plow through, but at least there is some resolve that I'm plugging along for my family. Little Emma won't have to talk about her suicidal aunt. Of course, years from now her playground friends will call me a killer. But her mother will set her straight. Maybe Emma will hear fond memories of me.

I finally fall asleep for a while, blessed relief that I didn't ask for. I dream that Brent is still alive, that we're hanging out at Malico's Pizza Plaza, eating pepperoni and whining about the forgetful waiter, as if his leaving off the sausage is the worst thing that could happen.

When I wake, Brent's gone again. I used to love Saturday mornings, but everything seems wrong in this moldy hotel room. I cry quietly as I shower and get ready to go to who knows where.

4

———

CASEY

If the police know I bought a ticket to El Paso, they might not be looking for me in Dallas. Still, I tie my bandana back on my head do-rag style and walk back to the bus station. I haven't decided where to go next, but the next bus is to Tulsa, Oklahoma, so I buy the ticket. I'm blissfully seated alone for most of the trip, and I fear falling asleep lest I miss the intermediate stops and go all the way to Tulsa. I have to get off somewhere along the way.

Durant, Oklahoma, seems as good a place as any. It's not an official stop, just a place where passengers have ten minutes to smoke or buy a Coke. I look around. We're not in a particularly good area of town, but I see a drugstore on a corner four blocks up. I walk with purpose, trying not to look like I'm lost. Even in the daylight, I could be a prime target—a petite blonde girl walking alone in a bad neighborhood.

I guess a person on the lam should be brave and bold, but I feel like a wilting tulip, my petals pointing to dirt. Fear pulses like blood through my veins again, in my ears, pounding in my head.

That's my brave girl, my dad used to say when I was ten in a new school, dealing with a bully who'd made my life miserable. I wasn't brave then any more than I am now. I avoided the mean girl in the hallway and stuck close to the teacher when she was around. Because I was new, I played alone on the playground, lip-synching to silent songs and smiling as though I hadn't noticed I was alone.

I smile now and move my mouth to that silent song, as if my mind is contented and preoccupied. No one seems to notice the falsehood in that expression or the tornado raging through my head.

No one really sees me at all.

I get to the drugstore and walk up the hair dye aisle. I stand in front of the L'Oreal products trying to decide what my new hair color will be. I've always liked being blonde, but any variation of that will look too much like me. No, I guess I'll have to go brunette. I grab a dark brown off the shelves, hoping I don't botch it.

I hear a crash and jump a foot. Someone at the front of the store curses. Catching my breath, I move along the center aisle until I can see up the row in front of the clerk. She's on her knees amid a toppled mound of acid reflux medication on sale two for one.

Without thinking, I rush toward her. "You okay?" I ask. "Did you fall?"

Her cheeks are flushed. "Yeah, I'm so clumsy. I knocked down the display." I reach out my hand to pull her up, and she takes it and gets to her feet. "Thanks. I can check you out if you're ready."

I glance up and see a security camera over the door. I lower my head. "Yeah, I'm ready. I can wait, though, if you need to pick them up."

"No, the display will wait."

Normally I would help her pick up the boxes. Small kindnesses used to cost me nothing. Now they're more expensive than I should be willing to pay. I follow her to the cash register, grabbing a candy bar and some nuts off the rack next to the counter, hoping to distract her a little from the hair color. "Hey, do you know of a safe motel around here? I'm just passing through town and I don't have a reservation."

She shoots the bar code of the hair color, the candy, the nuts, and drops them into a bag. "There's one up the street," she says, "but honestly, I wouldn't stay there if I were you. I would go farther into town, to the Hampton Inn on Burngard Street. It's a few miles from here, though."

"Do you mind if I use your phone to call a cab? It's not one of my better days. Car broke down and my phone battery's dead."

"Sure." She slides the store's phone across the counter. "Call information and ask for Dean's Taxi Service. They're the only ones in town."

I call for the cab, thank her, and wait outside, second-guessing every word I said to her. If she's questioned, she might remember me. But this is Durant, and they probably won't be looking for me here, at least not until I'm long gone. Maybe she'll never hear me called a murderer.

As I stand outside with my bag of hair dye, reality begins to drown me. What was I thinking? I should have called the police the second I found Brent, told them he was dead on the floor and who was surely to blame. But as quickly as that thought enters my mind, I know that it wouldn't have worked. My first instincts were right.

I wish I could see my mother and tell her everything, that she could hold me and reassure me that this won't smother me. I despise what this will do to her. She endured the lies and shocking grief before and emerged a different person—with shadows stretching dark through her soul and reflecting in her haunted eyes.

She still has my sister and my niece, who always bring a smile to those eyes. I can't stand the thought of not talking to them.

And I miss Brent. My confidant, the one who cared about the things from my past that plague me. Oddly, I still feel the impulse to pick up the phone and call him. Have they found him yet? Have his parents been told?

Is everyone who loves him wailing in grief right now?

Do they blame me?

Maybe they should, because his death is my fault. Guilt surges through me, and I don't know how to combat it. I just have to breathe and take the next step.

The Shreveport police aren't omniscient, and even if they get the state police involved, their reach is limited. But I know it isn't justice that will make them come for me. Justice has never had anything to do with it.

When the cab pulls up, the driver is a plump, gray-haired man with deep smile lines next to his eyes. I get into the backseat. "Thanks for coming," I say. "This probably isn't one of your usual pickup spots."

"No, ma'am," he says. "But I'll go most anywhere. How'd you get here?"

"Walked from the gas station," I say. "My car broke down, and it won't be fixed until tomorrow. I'm hoping the Hampton Inn has vacancies."

"Should," he says. "No weddings in town this weekend. So were you passing through?"

"Yes. I was going to Tulsa on business."

"Oh yeah? What do you do?"

I try to think of the least memorable job I can imagine. "I work for a company that designs cardboard boxes." I don't like how easily lying comes to me.

"Cardboard boxes?" the driver asks. "Never heard of that before."

I smile. "Yeah, well. Somebody's got to do it, right? You didn't think all those boxes just created themselves, did you?" I pause, wondering if I've gone too far. "How long have you been driving a cab?"

As I'd hoped, he moves on. "Three years. Lost my job when the plant closed down, couldn't get another one, so here I am."

"Doing what it takes," I say. "Good for you. You have a family?"

"Wife and daughter, and a sweet grandbaby. Daughter's not married, and at first I thought it was the end of the world. But that baby has us wrapped around her finger. Fifteen months old, and she's the joy of our lives."

"I love babies."

"Got any of your own?"

"No, but I hope someday. Got a picture?"

I'm not just trying to manipulate the conversation. I really love seeing people's family pictures, especially when there are babies.

He flicks on his phone and thrusts it back over the seat. I smile at the chubby face and laughing eyes. "She's adorable."

"God made them cute so we wouldn't send them back. There are long nights, but they're all worth it."

Soon we pull into the Hampton Inn parking lot. I hope I don't strike out here. "Thank you for the ride," I say. "Your granddaughter's a lucky girl."

I pay him, then get out of the car. The Hampton Inn does have vacancies, so I register under a fake name, claiming again to have lost my driver's license. When I tell them I want to pay cash, the desk clerk has to call the manager and clear it with him. He comes to the front and looks me over, then grants his permission. His scrutiny makes me nervous. When they give me the key, I take refuge in my room. The first thing I do is turn on the television to the national news, wondering if they'll have a story on the murder in Shreveport. It's doubtful, since the nation really doesn't care about one man murdered in a Louisiana town, no matter how amazing he was. While I listen to the news, I quickly color my hair. With my light base, I hope the color is dark enough. I wait the required fifteen minutes, then step into the shower and rinse it out.

As the color circles the drain, I think of all that blood. Brent . . .

I close my eyes and sink into the wet tub, shower water still running over me, and I let my grief have its way. I cover my mouth to muffle the rasping cries, and soon the spray grows cold. I turn it off and sit in the empty tub until I can breathe again.

When I'm finally able to move, I get out and dry my hair, surprised at the new person staring back at me in the mirror. I don't really have the right coloring for dark hair, but it is what it is. My eyebrows are still light, so I ignore the warnings on the directions and use what's left in the bottle to dab on my eyebrows, then lie flat on the bed, hoping it won't drip into my eyes. Instead of letting it run into my eyes when I rinse, I wipe it off with a damp washcloth. When I'm dressed again and my hair is dry, I stare at my reflection and don't recognize myself.

Yes, the eyes are still me . . . almond-shaped and a little too big for blending into crowds. Maybe they won't be noticeable if I keep going without makeup for a change—forsaking my beloved eyeliner. My glasses should help. They're kind of new and not too many people have seen them, so maybe they're safe.

Around eleven o'clock, I go down and throw the hair dye bottles and box away in a trash can at the end of the hall. Then I find the business center and get on the hotel's computer. I don't dare look at any of my friends' Facebook pages or e-mail them. Even checking the news in my hometown could give me away if police are watching for out-of-town logins. Maybe I'll check tomorrow right before I leave. That way, if they do happen to figure out where I am, I'll be on my way out. For now, I need Amtrak and Greyhound schedules. I have to figure out where to go next. I quickly find Amtrak, but there isn't a Greyhound station here. The closest one is in Ardmore, but I print it out anyway, along with the train schedule. I go back to my room and check my cash.

I have $12,000. When my sister and I were cleaning out my dad's things two years after his death, we found a stash of $36,000, money he'd saved a hundred bucks at a time over his whole career. It was in a box marked "Rainy Day." We gave it to our mom, and she insisted we divide it three ways. I've never touched it, never even put it in the bank. I kept it in a cigar box all these years, never sure what to spend it on. It almost seemed like blood money, since I wouldn't have had it without his death. Now I know it was my dad's provision for me, as if he'd known I would someday have to run from his enemies. It should be enough to get me hotel rooms and meals and possibly a new computer and phone. Maybe even an old used car when I get to where I'm going.

When I find a place to hide, I should get a job right away so I can stop drawing from it and replenish it.

Gratitude wells up in me that Dad had the foresight to leave us this. But he would have been horrified to know that I had to use it for this.

Halfway through the night, I'm still not able to sleep, so I sit up and think. I'll need a driver's license. You can't do anything without one. I go back down to the business office and hear voices at the desk, a woman and a man giggling and flirting. They haven't noticed me. I go into the small computer room and look up "fake driver's license."

Nothing helpful comes up on the screen. I guess people who break the law don't openly advertise. I go back to bed and try not to worry about it.

⌒⌒

Sleep finally comes, but I wake up early at seven o'clock, afraid that police are waiting in front of the hotel to catch me the minute I walk out the door. But that's silly. They wouldn't have waited. A SWAT team would have rammed down my door and bolted in with rifles aimed, ready to handcuff me and drag me away.

I go down to the business center and pull up a map on the computer and figure out how to get to the Amtrak station. I don't want to take a cab. I need the time to walk and clear my head. Before I leave the room, I quickly check a friend's Facebook page. He has been posting about me.

Someone appears at the glass door with their key card, so I quickly close out of that screen. I'll have to look it up again later.

I go back to my room and peel off a hundred-dollar bill to put in my pocket, and I still have some cash in my purse, but I divide the rest into two even stacks and put them into my boots.

Carrying my duffel bag, I walk blocks to the Amtrak station. On the way, I have to pass a man standing on a street corner. A drug dealer, maybe. He watches me as I approach. I fight the urge to cross the street and avoid him. In fact, it occurs to me that he can help me.

I slow as I come to him, and lift my chin like I'm not afraid. "How are you?"

He seems surprised at the question, his dreadlocks hanging heavy in the wind. "Just fine," he says, stretching the word *fine* out a little too long.

"I was just wondering if you could tell me, is there anyone around here who could help me get a driver's license?"

He narrows his eyes. "Tried the DMV?"

"Not a legal one." I feel the heat on my cheeks.

He nods, taking his time answering. "I might know somebody. Give me your number. I'll call you."

"I don't have a number," I say.

He nods again, as if he gets the fact that I'm trying to stay under the radar. "What's it worth to you?"

I pull out twenty dollars.

"Naw, that won't do it."

"Am I paying you for the license or the information?"

"The info, but it's worth something. How do I know you ain't a cop?"

"How do I know *you're* not?" I say.

He laughs then, and I notice molars are missing at the back of his mouth. "Sixty bucks'll get you to the right place."

I feel in my pocket for two more bills, pull them out.

He takes the money. "There's a diner on West Cedar Street. Pedro's Place, near the Taco Casa. Go up there and tell the dude behind the counter D.J. sent you. Tell him you're trying to find yourself."

Trying to find myself. I guess that's appropriate.

"Okay, thanks."

As I move away, he calls out, "You want any comfort, come back. I'll be here."

I need comfort; I know I do. But drugs have never been the answer.

Survival is all the comfort I can have for now.

5

CASEY

Not having transportation is getting old. I walk the two miles to West Cedar Street after asking a convenience store clerk for directions. It seems I'll never come to Pedro's Place. Was Dreadlock Guy just yanking my chain? It seemed too easy, and I'd expected to jump through more hoops. But it's not over yet.

By the time I finally see the neon sign, the money stacks in my boots are rubbing blisters. I step into the restaurant, grateful for the air-conditioning. "Help you?" a man who looks Hispanic asks.

I go to the counter and lean across it. "D.J. sent me. I'm trying to find myself."

The man looks me over as though in disbelief that I could need a new identity. After a moment, he turns away. "You want a menu?"

His turning away throws me. "What? No."

"We serve food here," he says in a heavy accent. "You want food, I get you a menu."

My heart races. "No, he said this was the place . . . where I could *find myself.*"

The man looks like he could spit nails. "You know this D.J. person?"

"No. I just met him. I asked him for help."

"Because he look so upstanding?"

I feel like I've been caught at something I haven't done yet. "No, because he didn't."

The honesty makes him stare again.

"I have money," I say quietly. "I can pay."

He keeps sizing me up, and I wonder if he thinks I'm a cop, like D.J. suggested. I suddenly feel exposed, as if he knows that my hair is recently dyed and my eyebrows are tinted, that I usually wear contacts and eyeliner, that I'm a fugitive from Shreveport police. But how could he know?

This is a mistake. I wave him off. "Never mind. I . . . changed my mind."

He lets me walk to the door, but just before I go out, he comes up behind me and whispers, "Back door. I meet you there and let you in."

Despite all my trouble to get here, now I'm not sure this is a good idea. Is he going to take me back there and make me wish I'd never met D.J.? I already do.

Still, I go—because I need a driver's license, and I have no other options. Running from the law makes you do surprising things.

My brave girl.

I go around back and wait at the door—my heart thumping in my chest—and finally he opens it. He looks both ways, then lets me in. I step inside. The room is more brightly lit than the dining room up front. A white cloth is duct-taped to the wall, and a camera is set up on a tripod.

"What do you need?" he asks.

"A new driver's license."

"Why?"

"Because . . . I need to start over." My voice rasps and grows weak.

"Your age?"

"Twenty-five," I say.

He goes through a stack of papers on his desk, stops at one, and pulls it out. "I have a twenty-five-year-old here, but it's a man."

"No," I say. "Has to be a woman." If this weren't so serious, I would laugh. "Also, I'd rather it wasn't somebody who could be hurt by this. Like, I don't want to steal anybody's identity. I just want a made-up name so I can get a place to live and stuff."

"You plan to work?"

"Yes, of course."

"Then you need social security card too." He flips through the pile, pulls another paper out. "Here . . . a twenty-six-year-old girl who died. Real person."

I catch my breath. "What did she die of?"

He looks at me like I'm an idiot. "I don't know what she die of. That is not my job."

"But . . . her family. If they find out someone's using her name . . ."

"Do you want new identity or not?"

I think about it for a moment. I don't like it, but what can I do? I have to start over somewhere, and if I don't have a social security number, I can't get a job.

"What's her name?"

"Grace Newland. Caucasion. Should work."

I can't get my mind off her death. "When did she die?"

"Two years ago, in Oklahoma City. You want or no? I have business to run."

I feel in some way like I was complicit in her death. "Can I see her picture?"

He is impatient. "I don't have her picture, lady. I will put *your* picture on the license. Your height and weight."

I stand there a moment, thinking through all the things a girl my age could have died from. A car accident? A disease? Foul play? I feel a sudden surge of grief, and tears burst to my eyes. "She died so young."

The man shakes his head like I'm a lost cause. He taps his watch.

"Okay," I say finally. "I'll be Grace Newland."

He moves me roughly in front of the backdrop cloth, snaps my picture. I don't have the chance to fake a smile. "Okay, it will be ready tomorrow morning."

"What? No, I need it now. I'm leaving town today."

"Too bad," he says. "I make tonight, have ready tomorrow. Take it or leave it."

I let out a long sigh, but like everything else, this is out of my control. "Okay, I'll take it."

"Five hundred dollar now, cash only. Other five tomorrow."

I nod, but I don't want to reach into my boot and show him my cash. "Do you have a bathroom I could use first?"

He points me to the one the employees use in the back, with cement walls and a bucket of dirty mop water in the corner. I go in and lock the door, pull off one boot, and count out five bills. Quickly, I put the boot back on.

The bills are damp and warm when I hand them to him, but he doesn't complain. He counts them, checks the digital picture in the camera one more time, then tells me to come back at seven thirty in the morning.

I leave Pedro's Place wondering if that was Pedro himself, or if Pedro is *his* alias. I feel a little bit hopeful that I've made one decision that will move me along this road. I hope he didn't just rob me. What will I do if he doesn't give me what I paid for? It's not like I can report him.

I remember passing a Holiday Inn Express on the way here, so I head back the way I came and stop in to get another room. One more night, and then I'll be on my way. I have to decide where I'll go.

I check in with cash again—using another name I come up with on the fly. I don't want to use Grace Newland yet because, if they track me here, I can't leave any clues about who I'll be from tomorrow on.

I look out the window of my room and spot a library a block away. I wonder if they have a computer I can use.

At the library, the air conditioner makes the place seem fresh and cool, and I find comfort in the smell of the books. I walk around, getting the lay of the land so I won't have to ask directions. I find the small computer room near the front door. There's a sign that says I need a pass to use the computer, so I go to the busiest clerk behind the desk and ask for one. She doesn't look at me, just hands me a small card.

I go into the computer room and glance around. There are twelve computers, four on each wall, and several people are staring at their monitors. A man sits at one in front of a screen of pornography. I quickly look away, but I can hear the offensive sounds.

I go to an empty chair and open the browser. I hesitate to get on Facebook, but the need to know what's going on with Brent's body compels me. The computer is old and takes a long time to load. When it finally gets to Facebook, the login screen comes up. I can't use my own account, so I create a new one. I think about my screen name. I don't want to use Grace Newland, so I look around for a random word

I can use. I see a sign that says, "Please don't leave children unattended."

Unattended. That word is as good as any, so I create the username with a random number beside it. It hasn't been taken, so I create a password and sign in as Un Attended.

A new profile page comes up, and Facebook prompts me to tell it every little thing about myself.

I'm wanted for murder and my hobbies are reading, traveling, and walking along the beach at sunset.

I give myself a much less interesting bio, then I go to my friend Carl's page. He's one of those who posts every thought that comes to his head, a picture of every meal he eats, every book he reads, every song he listens to, every item he buys.

He also accepts every friend request he gets without checking who they are. He was never popular in high school, so he sees having a large number of friends on Facebook as some kind of affirmation. Why pop his bubble?

Surely if he's heard about Brent's death, he'll be talking about it. He keeps his posts public, so I'm able to see that he's posted articles about me. My heart jolts. I scroll down to the first one, which links to the newspaper article dated yesterday. In his comment about the article, he has written: "I'm shocked and devastated by my friend Brent's death, but I can tell you without any hesitation that my friend Casey did not kill him!"

The words bring tears to my eyes. "Thanks, Carl," I whisper, smiling at his defense of me. I click on the article.

Brent Pace, 30, was found murdered in his home at 231 Ringbow Avenue last night at 9:00 p.m. Sources at the Shreveport Police Department say that he was stabbed six times and had been dead for several hours before he was found. Police are searching for Casey Cox, a friend of Brent's who may have information about the case. When asked if Cox was being considered as a suspect, police spokesman Joe McDonald said that she is a "person of interest."

The picture they've used of me is an old one that doesn't look much like me. I wonder where they got it. Did my mother or sister deliberately give them the one that least resembled me? Gratitude brings more tears, but I wipe them away so they won't draw attention to me. I know my well-meaning friends will be posting recent photos soon if they haven't already. Everybody will want to be part of the drama.

Behind me, a woman speaks to the man with the porn. "Sir, could you please use headphones or turn down the volume?"

He ignores her and keeps the volume where it is. The woman gets up and storms out.

I go back to Carl's page and click on the next article. It's a link to a video of this morning's local news broadcast of the same story. I don't want anyone to hear it, so I don't click on it.

A mother and a little girl about eight years old come in, and the mother parks the child next to me. She pulls up a YouTube channel she must have created for the girl. "Mommy'll be right out here if you need me," she says.

The little girl deftly clicks on the first video. It's something to do with a litter of kittens. I glance at the man whose monitor is visible if the child glances to her left. He's still viewing his smut, and the sounds grow even louder.

I slide my chair back and get up, lean over his computer. I jerk the power cord out of the back of the CPU. His display goes black and the sounds stop.

"What are you doing?" he says.

"An act of common decency." I wind the cord around my hand so he can't have it back. "There's a child in here."

"You can't do that. I can watch anything I want to on this computer."

"Fine," I say, going back to my chair. "Watch it."

He looks around at the other computers. The other users look uneasily at him, but some of them stifle smiles.

He bolts out, probably to report me, and some of the users turn to congratulate me. I don't answer, just focus on my screen. But when the man comes back with the librarian, I look for a wedding ring on his hand. Yes, there is one.

The woman checks his computer as if he hasn't already told her what happened. Next to me, the little girl giggles at a talking dog.

"She stole the power cord right off the computer," he says loudly. "Next, she'll steal the monitor and the CPU."

I can't escape the irony that librarians have the stereotype of being plain-Jane, wholesome bookworms whose favorite word is *Shhhh*, but now some of them are tasked with defending sleazy phlegm-wads' rights to view porn in public places. I hope that's not the case here.

I hand her the cord. "His computer was malfunctioning," I say. "I know his wife, and I'm pretty sure he wouldn't have been viewing porn deliberately."

The librarian blushes and turns back to the man. "Actually, sir, we have a policy prohibiting the viewing of obscene material."

The man looks suddenly embarrassed. Maybe he does have a conscience . . . or a healthy fear of his wife. He looks at me for too long, as if trying to decide if I really know her. He clearly decides not to chance it, then gives up and storms out.

The librarian thanks me and plugs the cord back in, then erases the history so his last website won't pop up accidentally for any eight-year-olds looking for puppies.

I realize how risky my actions have been. I should leave now. I've been seen, and people might remember me if they see me on the news. Why do I keep doing things that call attention to myself?

I wonder if the librarian, when she hears about me, will be more shocked that a fugitive was in the library than she was that a man was viewing porn in plain sight with a child present.

I shut down my browser, then step out of the room. I see the little girl's mother at a table, books open as she takes notes. She must be a student.

"Excuse me," I say. "There are people who watch pornography on the computers in there. You might want to stay with your daughter."

The woman looks shocked, and she gets up right away. "Right now? Did she see it?"

"No, I don't think so. But I thought you should know that it happens."

She grabs up her books and notebook and hurries to the computer room. "Thank you. I didn't realize . . ."

"I know. Who would think?"

I leave then and walk back to the Holiday Inn, wondering if someone has already spotted me and called the police. Why didn't I just stay in my room?

By now the police probably know I bought a ticket to Tulsa. They've probably checked every bus station stop between Shreveport and there. Would they also check the places we stopped to fill up for gas? Would Durant even be on their radar?

I stop at a McDonald's before going back to the hotel, get some food, and take it to my room to eat. My stomach rumbles at the first bite. I force some of it down, but I don't have much appetite.

I imagine how devastated Brent's mother must be. She must have so many questions.

Though I'm utterly exhausted, I have trouble sleeping. Dreams slash me, nightmares of finding Brent dead . . . the smell of death, the look on his face, the heart-stop of reality, the fear. His face morphs into my father's face, the smear of my father's blood on the floor . . .

Some people spring into action when they're in shock. I

freeze for way too long. After I found Brent, when I could finally move, I stumbled around, tracking footprints and DNA all over the place.

Of *course* I'm a person of interest. Why wouldn't I be?

I hope the man at Pedro's Place doesn't let me down tomorrow. I'm ready to move on. I just wish it were as easy as putting a dead stranger's ID in my wallet.

6

___

DYLAN

'm Dylan Roberts," I say, extending my hand to Brent's distant relative who stands at the door of the church. "I went to school with Brent. I think I met you at his graduation party."

"Yeah, I remember you," the dude says. "You two were pretty tight growing up. Heard you were in Afghanistan."

"Twice," I say. "Once in Iraq. Home now."

"Three deployments. What branch?"

"Army," I say.

"Still serving?"

I shake my head, though my Adam's apple feels trapped. "No, I'd had enough."

"Can't blame you, man. What are you doing now?"

I look toward the front, where Brent's parents stand shaking hands, their expressions tragic, devastated. His mother lived for her son. I imagine the news she got a couple of nights ago was like stepping on an IED.

I shake my thoughts back to the cousin. "I'm sorry, what?"

"Where are you working now?"

I hate that question. "Still looking for the right thing. Hey, I'm gonna go on up and talk to Mr. and Mrs. Pace. Good to see you again."

I can see that the cousin is torn up about Brent's murder.

Grief always baffles me. Mostly I avoid services like this, but Brent was my best friend not too long ago, and I couldn't just blow it off. I'm walking down the aisle as the music starts to play. Halfway down, I wonder if I should slip into a pew or stay the course. There's a line of about twenty people still waiting to be noticed.

I go on down and my gaze connects with Mrs. Pace. She surprises me by stepping out of the line and coming toward me. "Dylan . . . come here."

I blink back the sting in my eyes as I walk into her hug. She bursts into a fresh round of tears and whispers something I can't understand. I hold her like I would my own mother until she releases. When we finally separate and look at each other, I can't find a single word.

"I'm so glad you're back safe," she says, touching my face.

I nod, my throat closing again. "This is awful," I finally manage to say.

She can't answer, just nods, takes my hand, and pulls me through the cluster of people to her husband. Mr. Pace sees me and shakes my hand, then pulls me into another hug.

The preacher steps to the pulpit and asks people to take a seat for the prayer service, so I leave them there and go toward the back, looking for a seat. I'm glad so many have turned out for the Paces, but I'd rather be alone in this place.

I sit on a pew that's only halfway filled, and I stare toward the front of the room. It's not a funeral, since it's too soon. They're waiting for an autopsy, and it'll be days before they can bury him. Their church has turned their Sunday night service into a prayer service for the family. Will this just add one more stressful event to what promises to be a long mourning period, or will it be cathartic?

I suppose prayer is always a good thing, even when it hurts.

As the service begins with worship music meant to focus our thoughts on the One who gives life and takes it away, I can't manage to sing. Some stand. I lean forward in my seat, chin planted on the heel of my hand, and remember those days with Brent when we were kids, running through the creek bed and stirring up hornets' nests. Brent was always too curious for his own good.

I'm the one who was at war for three deployments. He's the one who wound up dead.

My survival is wrong on so many levels.

I sit through the service, praying as the preacher leads us for the comfort and peace of this family, for the police department to find the killer and bring that person to justice . . .

Sudden anger assaults me, and I feel the ceiling sinking, the walls sliding inward, enclosing me. I can't catch a breath, and my heart bangs against my chest. Sweat is clammy on my skin . . . I slip out of my pew and head outside.

The sun is beginning to set, and the air is crisp and clean. I settle my gaze on the trees surrounding the church and try to calm myself. The green lushness quiets my soul. There was so little green in those desert places halfway across the world. You would think it's safe here, that no bullets would penetrate glass front doors while breezes whisper through elms. But my body is on high alert, as if it could happen at any moment.

The doors of the church open, and I look back to see the father of another high school friend stepping out. He doesn't seem to notice me as he trots down the steps, but I call out. "Mr. Keegan?"

Gordon Keegan glances back at me. "Dylan! I didn't realize that was you, man. Thought you were off somewhere killing Taliban."

That flip statement grates, so I ignore it. "I'm home now. You still on the police force?"

"Sure am," he says. "I'm working this homicide, matter of fact."

"Really?" I step toward him, wondering if I should ask. "Do you guys know who did this?"

"We have a strong suspect, and she's skipped town."

She? "What's the deal? Was it a fight or what?"

"That's how it looks. He was stabbed six times in his home. Did you guys keep in touch?"

"Not for the last few years," I say. "We grew up together, but we'd lost touch. Was it a girlfriend? What's her name?"

He glances around; no one is near. "Keep this under your hat until we make an arrest. Reporters are buzzing about it, but I'd rather not confirm it. But did you know a girl named Casey Cox?"

I've never heard that name, so I shake my head.

"No, Kurt didn't either. She's a bit younger than you guys." Kurt is his son, also on the force.

"Did she have any priors?" I ask.

"None that we know of. Listen, I didn't tell you any of this. We're only calling her a person of interest for now."

"I understand," I say. "I saw Kurt last week when I was at the department applying for a job."

He looks intrigued. "That's right, you were a cop in the army, weren't you?"

"Criminal Investigations Division."

"Sounds like you'd be a great fit."

"Yeah, well, I don't think it's going to work out. But anyway . . ." My voice trails off.

"Well, I'll put in a good word for you."

I know it won't do much good. They have me marked as a victim of PTSD, and the force doesn't want to hire people who could snap. The CID had a problem with it, too, which is why I was discharged. It's the story of military life. They send you to places where bombs explode like jack-in-the-boxes, blowing your friends to pieces before your eyes. Then they punish you when you can't stop thinking about it.

"I hope you find the girl," I say.

"Yeah, me too," he says. "I kind of thought she might show up here, but we have a lot of people watching for her. She hit the road, but we're on her trail. We'll get her back here pretty quick."

I walk out to the parking lot with him, then sit in my car alone, staring as minutes pound by. I finally figure I could be praying, since that's what I came here to do.

Keeping my gaze on the whispering trees, I ask God why I had to lose yet another of my friends. Why does life have to hurt like a shrapnel wound in the center of your gut?

I ask him when he's going to plug up my holes and make me right again, before I wind up in the same state as Brent. Instantly, guilt pours through me. I should be praying for my dead friend's parents and that they find the girl and bring her to justice.

I whisper the words aloud, hoping God will hear even if my heart doesn't seem connected.

When I get back to my apartment, I don't bother turning on the lights. I sit in the dark, thinking. It occurs to me that I could go to a bar and get loaded or drown my thoughts in drugs. The VA doctors have given me enough scripts to get wasted for months. But numbing the pain doesn't buy my dead friends any justice. Brent, Blue Dog, Tillis, Unger . . . and all the others. If they had to suffer, why shouldn't I?

I won't take that path, because I don't want to add more wounds to the ones I already have. Escape is not an option.

But that leaves me here in the dark.

7

_____

CASEY

'm at Pedro's Place at 7:15 the next morning, my duffel bag in tow. I knock on the back door, and he doesn't answer. I consider going around front, but I don't want to make him mad, so I wait.

He opens the door at exactly seven thirty and looks out, first to the right and then to the left. Finally, he lets me in.

"Do you have it?" I ask.

He doesn't speak, just goes to an old beat-up desk in the corner and pulls an envelope out of a drawer. He thrusts it at me. "It is good work."

I open the envelope and pull out the driver's license and social security card of the dead girl. I wonder again how she died. I'm curious what she looked like, but my own face stares back at me. I'm once again startled by the color of my hair.

"Memorize social security. It is yours now."

"Thanks," I say. "You've helped me a lot." I look at him, waiting for him to meet my eyes, but he never does. "Just for the record, I'm not a bad person. I'm in trouble, but I didn't do what they think—"

He lifts a hand to stem my rambling. "I don't want to know your whys. Not my job."

"I know, but I'm not used to doing illegal things. I just wanted you to know I'm a decent person. I'm going to prove my innocence somehow."

"You never heard of me. Never saw me. Got that?"

"Yes . . . of course." I dig into my purse for the cash I've already pulled out of my boot, and pay him the rest of what I owe him.

He takes the cash, counts it out. Finally, he gives me a grudging look. "Did you eat?"

"No."

"I make you plate," he says. "You eat it back here."

I'm starving, so I smile. "You don't have to do that."

"Wait," he says and disappears to the front. His place smells like heaven on earth, and my stomach rumbles. While he's gone, I sit in a folding chair and examine my driver's license. It looks legit. I wonder how he does it, who he usually does it for. Illegal immigrants? Criminals? Innocents on the run, like me?

He comes back with a plate of eggs and hash browns, crispy bacon, and a biscuit smothered in gravy. He puts it on his desk, pulls his desk chair up to it, then motions for me to come eat.

"It looks so good," I say. "Thank you so much." I begin to eat, my salivary glands exploding with the taste.

"Good, yes?"

I smile at him. "Yes. I don't know when I'll get to eat again today, so this is perfect."

He watches me eat as if my pleasure gives him some satisfaction. Finally, he says, "I get back to work. You leave your plate here when you are done. Slip out back door."

I wipe my hands and reach out to shake. He holds my hand a second too long. "You've helped me a lot," I say. "I don't know what I would have done without—"

He stops me again. "Do not make me regret it," he says in a soft voice. "Don't do stupid."

I can't promise that, because I know myself, and I've already "done stupid" since finding Brent dead. He lets my hand go, then returns to the dining room. I finish up, wipe my mouth, then slip out the back.

My name is Grace Newland. I wonder if I could get away with going by Gracie, which sounds like Casey, but that's too close. I have to leave my name behind, and it hurts like another death. I've always liked my name. My dad gave it to me, and when he used it, it always preceded something profound.

Casey, humanity demands that you stand up for what's right.

Casey, there comes a time when you have to take risks.

Casey, I love you.

I'm not ready to say good-bye to Casey just yet. If I go far enough away, can I someday be her again?

8

___

DYLAN

When Brent's parents call me Monday morning to come visit, I figure they want me to be a pallbearer or do the eulogy or something. I hate the idea of speaking in front of a grieving crowd—calling attention to the tremor in my hands—but for Brent, I'll do anything they want.

Brent's family lives in a mansion. His father's family had all the money, though I never knew exactly what the source was. They never treated me like I was inferior, and at the ballpark when Brent and I played, they were just like everybody else.

I used to run through their house with Brent and slide

across their polished floors in my socks, and I don't remember them ever lifting their voices to us. His mother lived for her job as a stay-at-home mom, and she made Brent's life (and mine, when I was there) pretty idyllic.

That's why this seems surreal. Murder doesn't usually cross into well-to-do zones, and this family seems like they should be immune.

I suddenly feel awkward standing at the double front doors ringing the bell. Though I was invited, even summoned, I feel as though I'm imposing. A maid in a uniform opens the door and greets me. I tell her who I am, and she invites me in.

I wait in the foyer. When Mr. Pace comes to greet me, he has deep circles under his eyes, wrinkles etched like marionette lines from the corners of his mouth to his chin. In the light, I can see that he's aged more than his due. I wonder how many years this tragedy has stolen from him.

"Dylan, thank you for coming," he says. "Come on back."

I follow him through the dining room with its massive table and see the photographs of Brent laid out. "Elise has been going through his pictures. They want to blow some up for the funeral." His voice catches. "Don't even know when that'll be yet. We can't have his body until the autopsy is done. Like they need confirmation that the stab wounds were actually what killed him."

I hear the pain in his voice, even though his comment seems flip, but I get it. The morning after two of my buddies were killed right in front of me as we drove through Kandahar, the guys and I shared crude barbs about how the government would handle it. Humor in the face of grief is like opening a valve, letting some of the steam out before the whole thing blows.

There are relatives in the kitchen—cousins and aunts and uncles, grandparents sitting at the table. I smile and shake hands as Mr. Pace introduces me, but he walks on through, motioning for me to follow. He takes me to his study, a room previously off-limits to Brent and me. His wife is sitting in there by a window, looking out on the back lawn.

"Honey," Mr. Pace says in a soft voice. "Dylan's here."

She turns to me and I'm struck by her swollen eyes. "Thank goodness."

They motion for me to sit on the rich leather couch, and Mrs. Pace gets up and turns on lamps around the room. "Sorry about the dark. I don't know where my head is."

"It's okay," I say. "You don't have to turn them on for me."

"I know, but it's rude to invite someone into the dark. All these people in the house, I just needed to escape back here by myself. I love them, but I'm not myself today."

"No, of course not," I say. "Listen, Mr. and Mrs. Pace, I'm happy to do anything I can at the funeral. Whatever you need . . ."

They look at each other, then Mr. Pace says, "Call us Elise and Jim, Dylan. You're a grown man. We want you more as a peer now than as a friend of our son."

A peer? I'm not sure what that means now that our only connection is gone.

"Dylan, we want to hire you," Elise says.

I frown and sit straighter. "Hire me? For what?"

Elise defers to Jim, and he leans forward, his hands crossed between his knees. "This girl who killed Brent. She's skipped town, and we want you to help us find her."

My eyes narrow. "But the police are looking for her, aren't they? I ran into Gordon Keegan last night, and he said he's working on the case himself."

"He is, but now it looks like the girl has left the state, and the local police department's resources are limited. Too much time has already passed. We don't want to leave it strictly in the hands of the police department."

There's a knock on the study door, and I look up as Jim calls, "Come in."

Speak of the devil. Gordon Keegan and his partner, some detective I don't know named Rollins, come in. Handshakes all around. Keegan is much more grim and subdued than he was last night. Elise pours them coffee, then sits them down in chairs across from the couch where I sit.

"I was just telling Dylan that we need some help."

Keegan sips his coffee. "It's not that we can't find her. We'll be looking ourselves, and we have plenty of resources. But she's smart. She's not using her credit cards, her phone isn't pinging off any towers. She's not in her car. After the media broadcasted what kind of car it was, someone saw it in a hotel parking garage and called it in. We know that she bought a bus ticket to El Paso, but she got off in Dallas. We're pretty sure she bought another bus ticket to Tulsa, but she didn't make it there. The driver remembers her and thinks she got off in Durant. We think she may still be there."

"What can I do?" I ask.

"We want to hire you as a private investigator," Jim says. "We'll pay you more than you were making in the army, plus expenses. We want you to help us track her down."

My heart begins to race. "So . . . the police department is hiring me?"

"No," Keegan says too quickly. "The family is paying you, but the department is on board with it. We've had budget cuts lately, so the city can't afford to fly us all over the place looking for this girl. Since the Paces are willing to pay, it works out for all of us to outsource this. We want her back as soon as possible."

I set my coffee cup down. "I didn't know this kind of thing happens. Do I need a PI license or something?"

"You already have a license from working with the Army Criminal Investigations Division."

"Yeah, but I've been discharged."

"Honorably. We'll give you consultant credentials. That should be enough."

I don't mention that my PTSD was a red flag to the department when I applied for a job, but Keegan brings it up.

"Listen, I know the chief was hard-nosed when you tried to get on with the force, but since this is a privately funded thing, it's different. And if you find her and bring her back so we can prosecute her, it'll look good for you. It'll be a chance for you to prove yourself. If all goes well, I don't think there's any way the chief wouldn't want to hire you after that."

That sounds good. And honestly, I have nothing better to do. "I'm honored that you'd think of me, Mr. and Mrs. Pace."

"Jim and Elise," Elise says again. "Say yes, Dylan. We know you loved Brent. We know you were good at your job. We trust you to do everything possible to find this girl who took Brent away from us."

I think through my schedule. I have a shrink appointment Thursday, a group therapy Friday, a Bible study on Sunday, and a job interview with UPS—as a deliverer—sometime next week. I don't want to deliver packages, though. I want to be a cop.

"I can write you a check right now," Jim says. "We can get you a chartered flight to Durant today. I've talked to a pilot friend of mine, and he can fly you there at four o'clock this afternoon. Commercial flights don't fly in there, but they do have a small private airport. That was the soonest I could get you out."

I look at Keegan and his partner. "If I agree to this, I'll need to go over the evidence you have. I want to see the crime scene. The pictures." My stomach pitches at the thought of seeing my friend murdered, but I've seen dead friends before. "I want everything you have on the girl. I'd like to interview her family before I leave."

"No, that would tip them off that you're looking for her," Jim says. "I don't want them warning her."

"Do you have their phones tapped? Their computers, e-mail, Facebook?"

Keegan nods. "The DA gave us a warrant for that within a couple hours after Brent was found. She hasn't contacted them, from what we can tell."

"Can you do it, Dylan?" Jim asks.

I think for just a moment. How can I say no? This is Brent we're talking about. "Sure, I can do this. What do you want me to do when I find her?"

"Contact local police and have them go with you to arrest her," Keegan says. "We'll have her extradited here."

I look at my watch. It's 11:00 a.m. "Do you have time to go over everything with me?" I ask Keegan.

"Sure," he says. "Let's get started right now. We'll meet at the department."

Elise gets tears in her eyes as she stands up with me. She hugs me and touches my face again, as if she hopes I'll morph into her son. "I feel secure knowing you're on the case, Dylan. Let's get justice for our boy."

As I follow the two detectives out, I sincerely hope that I don't let these people down.

9

CASEY

I go back to the hotel and get on their computer and look up a Google Earth picture of the Amtrak station. There's a hotel a block from it. I can get a cab to drop me off there in case he's questioned later.

I catch a cab out front and ask the driver to take me to a convenience store and wait for me. I get a few snack items for my trip and a baseball cap. I don't think I've ever worn one in my life, but it seems like the prudent thing to do if I'm going to walk through an Amtrak station where there will be cameras. I get back into the taxi and ask the driver to take me to the hotel. I'll walk the rest of the way to the train station.

This cabbie is quiet, not at all interested in me. I'm grateful. When we arrive, I pay him and go into the lobby, use the restroom, then walk down to the station.

I quickly spot security cameras at every corner and over the ticket counter. I keep my head down, shielded by my cap, and examine the schedule. There are trains leaving every hour. The next one is going to Houston. I see security guards at the doorways, and I glance at those cameras again.

This won't work. If I buy a ticket here and someone's watching for me, they'll know exactly where I'm going, even if I get off at a stop along the way. Security cameras will catch me wherever I disembark.

But Greyhound doesn't have a bus station in Durant. If they did, we wouldn't have filled up at a gas station, would we?

A frazzled woman with three kids walks past me, and I tap her shoulder. She turns.

"Excuse me, do you live in Durant?"

She nods and grabs her preschooler's hand. "Yes."

"I was wondering—is there a bus station here? Like Greyhound or something?"

"Not Greyhound, but there is a Trailways," she says. "It's three blocks over from here, I think."

I thank her, compliment her kids, then head out the door. As I walk in the direction she pointed, I hope she's not one of those directionally challenged people who doesn't know north from west. I head in the direction she sent me, and in three blocks, I see the station.

Bus stations aren't usually high tech or secure, probably because they don't serve as many people and have to keep their costs down. I go in, bill of my baseball cap down, and study their schedule on a TV screen on the wall. There's a bus going to Chicago, one to Atlanta, and one back the way I've come, going through Shreveport and down to New Orleans, all in the next three hours. I think for a minute. Where are they most likely to think I'd go?

I have an aunt who lives in Belleville, Illinois, so they would probably expect me to go toward Chicago. Cousins in Texas and Louisiana, so they'd probably check out the stops on the way to New Orleans.

I have some relatives in Alabama, but I hardly know them. Risking going east, I choose Atlanta. I don't have to wind up there. I can start there and decide whether to get off along the way or go even farther. The main thing is that I'll be tucked away while I travel.

I go to the window, buy the Atlanta ticket. It doesn't leave for two hours, so I have time to kill. I long for my phone or my computer. I'll buy one when I get where I'm going, but not yet. The fewer clues I leave, the better.

I have the sudden urge to call Brent and tell him about the driver's license and social security card, and the brusque man at Pedro's Place turning nice on me. But Brent's not there.

My eyes burn, but I know crying will call attention to me, so I go back into the bathroom. I wash my face in the sink, wipe my eyes, then realize how dirty the bathroom is. I have nothing to do, so I pull out some paper towels and wipe the counter, pick up the stray wads of paper towels around the floor, pull out the garbage bag and tie it up. I find a roll of new bags at the bottom of each trash can and reline them.

I leave the bags of garbage against the wall for the janitor to find. Maybe it'll brighten his day.

When I was a little girl, I was a Brownie for about two years, and there was a story in the handbook about a stressed-out mom of two bratty girls whose house was a mess, and when she got up one morning, the house was spotless. No one could solve the mystery of who'd cleaned the house, and it happened several days in a row. At the end of the story, you learn that it was her bratty children who'd done it. They weren't such brats after all.

A plump woman comes in while I'm cleaning, and she opens a stall, sees that the toilet is stopped up, then comes back to me. "Ma'am, this one over here is clogged."

I smile at her. "I don't work here. I'd fix it if I knew how, but . . ."

She seems embarrassed. "I'm so sorry. I thought you did. You were cleaning."

"Yeah, just burning off some energy."

"Well, isn't that nice?" She chooses another stall. I quickly wash my hands and decide to get out of here before she memorizes my face.

They say no good deed goes unpunished, and that's never been more true than in my case. I blend back into the travelers and wait it out as unobtrusively as I can.

I'm one of the first on the bus, so I choose two rows in front of the bathroom. I want to be far enough back that no one notices me, but not at the absolute rear, in case I want to lean my seat back a little. I'm hoping the bathroom smell won't reach to this row.

As the bus fills up, every row is taken, but people are still getting on. I put my earbuds in, again not attached to anything, and sit in the aisle seat with my eyes closed. If I don't make eye contact with anyone, maybe no one will want to sit with me.

But that's too much to expect. I open my eyes when I sense someone stopping at my row. It's the woman I spoke to in the bathroom, the one who saw me cleaning. She smiles down at me apologetically. "I'm sorry to wake you up, honey. Do you mind me sharing with you?"

I don't want to make her feel bad, so I mumble, "Of course not," and scoot over, sliding my bag with me. I put my feet on it since there's no leg room.

The woman is about the age my grandma would be if she'd lived. The long trip is probably going to be hard on her. She has a sweet expression on her face, every line etched into her leathery skin indicating that it came from smiling.

"My name's Lucy," she says.

"Hi, Miss Lucy. I'm . . ." I stumble on my name. "Grace."

"Beautiful name," she says. "I had a sister named Grace.

She passed away three years ago. Heart attack, but she had a good life."

"I'm sorry," I say. "It must be hard to lose a sister."

She nods. "Yes, but there are worse things."

I can't read whether she wants to tell me what those worse things are, but I have a few clues in my own life. "Are you going to visit family in Atlanta?" I ask her.

"Not Atlanta, really. My daughter, who lives in Shady Grove, is picking me up there. I'm going to live with her and my grandchildren."

"Oh, that's nice," I say. "How many grandchildren do you have?"

Her smile fades. "I have three, a girl and two boys. Ten, twelve . . . and sixteen." Her voice catches when she says *sixteen*. She looks away, her expression melancholy. I sense that she doesn't want to talk anymore, so I lean my head against the window and look out.

The bus driver gets on, and we pull out of the Trailways lot. Miss Lucy seems lost in her thoughts, and when I glance at her, her eyes are sad as she looks out the window at the town she has probably called home for most of her life. It occurs to me that she's saying good-bye like I had to, maybe for the last time, if she's going to live with her daughter. I feel guilty that I didn't let her have the window seat, but I thought I was doing her a favor by letting her have the aisle.

I fall asleep for real, finally satisfied that no one's going to kick the door in and cuff me. But my sleep is fitful, and I dream terrible snippets of dreams. Blood . . . stab wounds . . . skin the color of death . . . the sinking certainty that Brent's gone forever.

I wake up in a jolt, damp with sweat. Miss Lucy isn't there. I look around the bus to see if she's changed seats, but I don't see her. Her bag is still there, under the seat. In a moment she returns from the bathroom, slips back in. "Oh, you're awake. I hope I didn't wake you when I got up."

I try to smile. "No, not at all."

She stands again to let me out to go to the bathroom, keeps standing until I get back so I can slide in.

"So are you going to see family in Atlanta?" she asks, parroting the question I've already asked her.

I think of making something up, but I don't have the energy to lie. "No, ma'am," I say. "I don't know anybody there."

"A job?" she asks.

"Not yet." I know I'm going to have to explain something. "I'm kind of leaving a bad situation. Just want to go somewhere new and start over."

She nods as if that makes all the sense in the world, as if I just used secret code. "I had an abusive husband when I was your age," she says, lowering her voice. "Violent, violent man. Back then, you didn't just up and leave when you weren't happy in your marriage. But when he turned on my daughter, I had no choice."

"Did you divorce him?" I ask.

"No," she says with a ragged sigh. "I killed him."

10

DYLAN

I learned in the army to pack fast and light, so it doesn't take me long today. I throw the things I'll need for a day or two into my bag, then hurry to the police station where Keegan and his partner are waiting for me. As they pull out the crime scene photos and lay them out like cards on the warped conference table, I have to pull back for a moment, close my eyes, and remind myself that I am not here as Brent's friend. I'm here as a criminal investigator.

My brain shifts gears as I study the photos. "His body is lying on the bottom three stairs," I say. "Looks like he fell backward when he was stabbed."

"Right," Keegan says.

"So did the girl have a key? Was there any sign of forced entry?"

"No sign of forced entry; we don't know if she had a key or not. She might have rung the bell. They could have been talking at the bottom of the stairs. Or maybe she'd been there for a while and had just come downstairs with him when they got into a fight."

I'm quiet for a moment, studying the other pictures and the stab wounds on his body. The stabs are vicious and calculated, not just hastily thrown jabs in a fit of anger.

"How big is the girl?"

"About five three, hundred fifteen pounds."

Quiet again, I study the cuts. They weren't just jabbed, they were also pulled, causing the most amount of lethal damage. "Do we know how deep the cuts were? How wide?"

"We don't have the autopsy report yet."

"Can I call the ME and talk to him?"

Keegan looks at his partner, clearly irritated. Maybe I'm overstepping my bounds.

"If you have time before your flight, sure, but I don't know how that will help you find the girl."

"What about motive?" I ask. "Were they dating? Was it a fight?"

"That's what we think so far," Keegan says. "But you know what? We don't need a motive. We have the murder weapon."

My eyebrows go up. "You found the knife?"

"In her car," Keegan says.

"She didn't even try to dispose of it?" I ask.

"Apparently not. She just got out of town as fast as she could."

"What kind was it?"

Rollins speaks up. "Deer Hunter Stiletto with a five-inch blade."

I frown, thinking. That doesn't sound like something a woman would own, so more than likely she bought it just to kill Brent.

Keegan pulls a picture of the knife out of the stack, lays it on top. I study it and the rest of the photos. "I'm not sure of Louisiana's statutes on chain of custody of crime scene photos, but can you give me copies?"

Keegan stares at me. "Why?"

"So I can study them. I'll need to refer to them later."

"For what?" Keegan asks. "Dylan, you're tasked with finding her. That's all. Not with any other part of the investigation. And the last thing we need is for these to show up on Facebook. These are sensitive photots, and I don't want his family seeing them."

Heat rushes to my face. "You don't have much faith in me if you think I'm so unprofessional that I'd upload these to social media and show his parents . . ." I stop and modulate my voice. "I was a cop, Detective. Not some moron with a gun. If I'm part of this investigation, I want to do it right."

Keegan doesn't look convinced.

"I'm only hoping to get inside Casey Cox's head," I say as I point to one of the pictures. "The angle of these knife wounds can tell me a lot about her state of mind. The location of Brent's body gives us clues to what was going on minutes before. If I can piece these things together, I'll be able to think like she thinks. That's how I work."

Keegan's eyes narrow. "Just bring her back, Dylan."

I note a period at the end of his sentence, so I give up and change the subject. "I'd like to see Casey's place before I leave. It might give me clues about her intentions."

"Right," Keegan says. "I'll take you there now if you want."

I look at the photos again, taking in all I can. I want to know more about Brent's house. I haven't been there since he moved in, and I need to have a sense of the scale of the place. I check my watch. "I have plenty of time before I have to be at the airport. I'd like to go by the crime scene too. Is the house still sealed?"

"Yeah, but we've already processed the scene," Keegan says, opening another file. "We've logged all the evidence against the girl. We have a rock-solid case. Her DNA is all over the place. Shoe prints, fingerprints, the weapon . . . She did it."

"Again, I just want to get into her head," I say. "If she's determined to stay hidden, I need to get a step or two ahead of her."

Rollins, Keegan's partner, nods. "Sure, we can take you by there. Which do you want to do first?"

"Crime scene," I say. "Then her place."

"My guess is you'll find her tonight and have her back here by morning," Keegan says.

"Hope so." But I know how these things go. If she's fighting for her life, she won't make it easy for us.

We take the short drive to the crime scene. As we approach the small Victorian house, I can't help wondering if Brent's mother found the house and bought it for him. It looks like her. I imagine her coming to him all excited. *"I've found the perfect house for you. You'll love it. Come on, sweetie, you have to see it right now."*

Brent was like any other guy I know. As long as he had a TV, a game console, and a mattress—not necessarily on a bed frame—he was good. But his mother had loftier ideas for him. I can't picture him house shopping with a real estate agent. No, he would have let his mother do that for him.

My mind flashes back to his bedroom in that big house when he was growing up. His mother had paid a decorator big bucks to design the perfect boy's room. It was painted deep purple and had gold curtains—LSU colors—and his bedspread was an LSU tailgating blanket. His choice.

We had beanbags thrown on the floor in front of his TV, where we spent long hours playing video games. He had a small fridge in his room that his mother stocked with Gatorade and Coke. We spent most of the time on the floor, though there were high-end easy chairs.

I wonder if he still has those beanbags.

Had. I correct myself and force my brain back into gear. I'm not a grieving friend. I'm an investigator.

I follow the two detectives to Brent's door, slip on the blue shoe covers and gloves they offer me, and when they unlock it, I duck under the tape across the door keeping people out. The stairs where he was found are in the foyer, just five feet from the front door.

There is still plenty of dried blood on the floor where it bled out of him. I'm sweating now, and my heart hammers in a weak staccato beat. I force myself to think like a cop. I study the blood splatter on the wall. There are drops on the bottom quadrant of the wall close to the stairs, but I see a couple circled closer to the door, suggesting that the first time he was stabbed may have been as the person came in. Risking Keegan's wrath, I take quick pictures on my phone. He doesn't stop me, probably because his body's not in these shots. The stab wound across his carotid artery was too high for Casey to have landed easily, since Brent was considerably taller than her.

I see the small footprints in the blood on the floor and stairs. Looks like a knee print right next to his body, then shoe prints. One of the prints slides, as if she slipped but caught herself. She certainly wasn't trying to cover her tracks.

I take a picture of those prints, though I know they're among the ones I've already gotten. Keegan doesn't stop me this time either.

When I've gotten enough, I step into the dining room that

his mother clearly decorated. I have to hand it to her. It's masculine, but still with her slightly feminine touch.

From there, I go into the kitchen. "It's spotless."

"Yeah, not a dish out. Word is he ate out a lot. Didn't do a lot of cooking. Few dirty glasses in the dishwasher."

"Can I go upstairs?"

"Yeah, just stay to the side of the stairs."

I don't have to be told that. Though they've pretty much finished processing the scene, they wouldn't still have it sealed if they didn't think they might have to come back. I carefully walk up the stairs, noting that there's no blood above where his body was found. Had he come down to answer the door? Had the killer charged him when he did?

There are two bedrooms. I check the master first. One side of the king-sized bed is neatly made, but the side where he slept is rumpled and the covers are thrown back. He must have slept alone.

I look around, see his watch on the dresser, some change, his phone charger plugged into the wall. I step into his bathroom. It's clean, and his razor is on the sink, next to a bar of soap and some mouthwash. A few of his other items are on the vanity, and in the shower are the usual items, including a washcloth now dried to the consistency of cardboard.

No sign that the killer came up here after the murder. I glance into the guest room. The bed is made and there are no personal items on the tables or dresser.

When I go back down, I circle through the living room.

There they are—the beanbags we used to sit in. Though the room is decorated with masculine comfort—he didn't let his mother get too fussy with the decorations in here—he still has those beanbags in front of the TV screen. The newest-model game console sits on the media cabinet.

I look around, trying to figure out if the killer came in here at all. There's no blood on the floor, no bloody prints on the door casing. "What all did they log? Was there a computer? Any papers out? Bills? Letters?"

"Yes. There was a stack of bills on the kitchen counter that we took in. We got his laptop and a desktop computer. His phone."

"Can I get a copy of the evidence log?"

Keegan gets that look again. "No, you can't." He checks his watch. "We'd better get moving if we're going by the girl's apartment."

I decide not to fight. I'll just go through the evidence clerk at the department, and through Mr. Pace, I'll get the chief to approve my access to what I need.

I do a quick run-through of the house one more time, taking more pictures.

When I'm back in the car, I'm silent in the backseat as I try to work through what must have happened. He was upstairs alone, and he heard the doorbell. He trotted down the stairs to answer it. The person—Casey Cox?—stepped inside and stabbed him. With the wound under his ribs, maybe she hit him first, then when he doubled over, she could have gotten his neck. He would have stumbled back, fallen to the bottom three stairs. Otherwise, the stab wounds to his chest seemed too high if she was only five-three. Brent was an inch taller than me, at least six feet.

I think about the amount of blood she slipped in. For that to happen, she had to have gone in, kept stabbing, and stayed there for at least a few minutes. She didn't just stab and run.

Why would she do that? A person who had purchased a knife to kill him, who was planning before she rang the doorbell to stab him, who had the knife poised as he opened the door. Wouldn't she kill him, then take off before she had time to step in the blood? Why would she wait for it to pool on the floor, then kneel next to him and walk through it?

His wallet was still upstairs on his dresser, so it wasn't theft. It wasn't likely that he had anything of value on him since he'd probably just come from upstairs.

"Have you considered that someone else could have done the stabbing, then this girl discovered him?" I say aloud, though I'm still just thinking it through.

"Then why wouldn't she call the police?" Keegan asks. "Why would she run? She did a number of things consistent with guilt."

"How long had they been seeing each other?"

"We've interviewed a number of their friends," Rollins says. "They all say they weren't officially dating, that they were just close friends."

"Any history of fighting?"

"No one had ever seen them fight."

"What about the girl? Any history of mental illness?"

There's a pause, then Keegan glances back at me. "The girl . . . Casey . . . discovered her father's body after his suicide when she was twelve. I knew the guy. He was on the force. Nice guy, nobody had a clue he was depressed or anything like that. Anyway, she was probably traumatized by that. Had therapy for a couple of years as a kid."

I lean up. "Wait. So you *know* this girl?"

Keegan shakes his head. "No, I don't know her. I mean, I interviewed her back then, after it happened, but she was just a kid. She was a mess. But I haven't seen her in thirteen years or so."

I make a mental note to learn everything I can about that suicide. "Was she on medication?"

"Not that we can tell."

"Any priors?"

"None. Not even a traffic ticket."

"So why would a person like that snap and stab a friend to death?"

Keegan laughs then. "Who knows why anybody murders? My guess is she's been mental all these years and it just now manifested itself. Maybe Brent had another girlfriend and she lost it. We're digging in to all that."

There's more, I think. I need to talk to her friends myself. I need to learn about her relationship with Brent, how long they'd known each other, what kinds of things they did together, how close they were. How she did relationships. Was she transparent and easy to get to know, or aloof and hard to crack?

Were there signs that she could be homicidal? Did she have PTSD symptoms that made her react illogically and wildly to situations that didn't warrant it? Did certain things trigger flashbacks to her discovery of her dead father?

I suppose if she had an extreme case of PTSD, coupled with other mental disorders, it's possible. But it doesn't seem likely. I've been that person who reacted violently to someone waking me from a deep sleep, and I occasionally vomit or break out in a heavy sweat when I hear a loud noise. But I can't imagine selecting a knife, driving to someone's house, and stabbing him. That's premeditated, not a reaction to a mental trigger.

Wouldn't there be subtle signs that she had this in her?

We arrive at her building, a big old house apparently divided into six apartments. Hers is sealed with crime scene tape, like Brent's. Keegan has the key, so he opens it and we duck under the tape.

The apartment is small and relatively neat. She's lived here long enough to make it homey. She has decorated the walls with art and family pictures, but no pictures of herself. The kitchen and living room are combined; an area rug marks the living area where she has a couch and two easy chairs.

I see a check on the Formica counter. "What's this?"

"Rent check," Keegan says. "Dated the day of the murder."

"She left rent before she skipped town?"

He points to a note she left under the check. "Read that."

I move the check and see the note written in a neat script. Short and sweet. "Mr. Criswell, you can give my stuff to Goodwill if my mother doesn't come to get it in the next few days."

"So she wrote it after the murder and before she left town. Probably didn't want to alert him she was leaving before she was on her way."

"She knew we'd be here," Keegan says. "She didn't even try to clean up after herself."

He points to the bloody print on her floor, with a marker next to it indicating what number it is on the evidence log. I take a picture of it, then study the pattern. "Do we know the kind of shoe that is yet?"

"Yeah, Skechers. Same exact pattern as the ones at the crime scene."

"Did she call anyone before she left?"

"Just a cab. Got out of Dodge fast as she could. Took the next bus out as far as we can tell."

"So she might not have had friends in Durant? It might have just been a random trip to evade authorities?"

"The bus left around two," Keegan says. "Body wasn't discovered until nine that night."

"What was the time of death?"

"Around ten a.m."

I do the math. "So there were four hours between the murder and the bus? Weren't there other buses out earlier than that?"

"Yes, but we don't think she got to the station before about one."

"Why? What would she have been doing in the meantime? She didn't bother to clean up the crime scene or her apartment."

"Maybe she was driving around trying to figure out what to do."

"Where's her car?" I ask.

"At the lab. It was found in a hotel parking lot downtown. It has bloody footprints, too, blood on the door handles, inside and out on the driver's side."

I try to imagine what a person who'd planned a murder might do afterward. If she had gone over to Brent's to kill him . . . if she'd lunged at him just inside the front door . . . if she had inflicted those wounds and made sure he was dead . . . wouldn't she have had a plan for escaping more quickly afterward?

As I walk through her apartment, my mind works through the puzzle. It doesn't fit together. I mentally pull it apart as I stand in her bedroom, then put it back together another way. If she wasn't the one who killed him . . . if she had discovered him a couple hours after his death, then rushed home to get some things and leave . . .

I'm not sure which makes more sense, but I don't want to leave any stones unturned.

"Where does she work?" I ask as I move through her rooms.

"Insurance company. She does clerical work. Coworkers say she never said a word about leaving, and no sign of snapping like this. She left Friday for lunch and never came back."

Her bedroom is relatively neat. She has a style, one my sister would call shabby chic, but her furniture pieces fit nicely together, and the decor on the walls, the curtains, the arrangement of pictures and knickknacks on her shelves all seem comfortable and warm.

But killers can have nice homes, too, so that means nothing.

Still, as I look around, I don't see signs of her being a homicidal maniac, someone who could stab a man to death.

"The CSIs logged her computer?"

"Yes."

"Would it be possible for me to get a copy of her hard drive? I'd like to see if there are clues to her whereabouts in her e-mails."

"I told you, she's in Durant."

"But you said you weren't absolutely sure. And if she is, where in Durant? Her e-mails could help."

Keegan looks at his partner. "I'll have to check on that. Our lab works on its own timetable, and getting them to hurry with things is like pulling teeth."

"If they don't want to give me the whole hard drive, they could just give me her e-mail. If it's a server I can get to online, just the login info will do."

"I'll see. Doubtful we can get it done before you leave town."

"Maybe if I talk to them?"

Keegan gives an irritated laugh. I've overstepped again, but I hold my ground. Either I'm going to do this job right or I'm not. "If she's already left Durant when I get there, I'll need to know where to go next. Her e-mails could give me clues."

Rollins speaks up. "I'll talk to the lab, see what we can do."

"Good," I say. "I can read them on the plane." I take pictures of every wall of her apartment, every footprint the CSIs have marked, every surface, every framed picture. Keegan doesn't balk. Then I turn back to them. "Can I see her car before I go?"

Keegan checks his watch again. "I really think you need to get to the airport, Dylan. It's getting late."

He's right, but I've already learned things about her from being here. Like the fact that she doesn't seem to be a narcissist. She's in a few group photos she left behind, but mostly her pictures are of others. And she took care to pay her rent before she left. That tells me she has enough empathy for her landlord to suggest that she's probably not a psychopath.

I walk to a shelf and point out a photo with several people in it. "That picture there, it's Brent, isn't it?"

Keegan squints and goes toward it. "Yeah, I guess it is. The CSIs didn't log that. There were several other pictures of him that they did log."

"So she has pictures of him all over her house. It just doesn't make sense that she would show up at his house with a knife in her hand if she cared a lot about him."

"She was obviously a mental case obsessed with him." Keegan taps his watch again. "You need to get to the airport soon, Dylan."

I look back at the place, wishing I could stay longer. I'd like to sit in her easy chair and see what she sees each night when she's alone. I'd like to go through her drawers and cabinets, see what clues I might find there.

But the longer it takes me to get to Durant, the more time she'll have to hit the road again. Reluctantly, I follow them back out.

When we get to the bottom floor, her landlord steps out of the door marked "Manager." He's an older man with a hearing aid in his ear, and he has a grieved look on his face. "Have you found Casey yet?" he asks.

"Not yet," Keegan says. "You haven't heard from her, have you?"

"No. I would let you know."

"We'll be unsealing the apartment in a few days," Keegan says. "You'll be able to clean it up and rent it out—and cash that check she left."

"I don't care about that," he says. "I'm just worried about her." His eyes mist over. "She's a good girl, that Casey. Sweet. Always thinking of others. She could never have done what they're saying."

I take it all in, thinking that I might call him later and pick his brain.

"Thank you, Mr. Criswell. We'll be in touch when we unseal the apartment. Please do call us if you hear from her."

As we get in the car, I look up at Casey's second-floor windows, wishing I had time to interview the neighbors, the people at nearby stores, the employees she worked with, her boss. It would be helpful to know their experiences with Casey.

My adrenaline pumps as we head to the airport, and I feel a sense of purpose again. It feels good. I haven't felt it since I was discharged.

Part of me hopes I'll find her right away, and of course, I'll do all I can to make that happen. But the other part would like to stretch it out. I'd love nothing better than to be right in the middle of this case, with full access to everything regarding Brent's murder.

For now, I'll do my part, one puzzle piece at a time.

11

_____

CASEY

What Miss Lucy said—that she killed her husband—seems even more shocking than what police will say I did. I gape at her. "You *what?*"

"It was self-defense. He was drunk and was beating my baby girl. She was only seven. When I tried to stop him, he came at me. I went to the bedroom and grabbed his hunting rifle and . . . shot him."

I'm stunned, and I can't think of anything to say.

"I don't know why I told you that," she says. "I never talk about that to anybody. You must think I'm terrible."

"No, no," I say quickly. "Did the police come?"

"Yes, I called them the minute it was over. They saw Sandra's injuries—and mine—and it was pretty clear what happened."

"Did they give you a hard time?" I ask.

"Tried to at first, but the grand jury wouldn't indict me. He went too far."

"That's terrible."

She shakes her head, as if shaking herself out of her thoughts. "I don't know why I told you that," she tells me again. "Maybe it's just leaving Durant that has me going back in time. That town was good to me for the most part."

"Did you ever marry again?"

"No. After that, I was happy to live alone with my daughter. It's a hard thing, taking a life, even if he deserved it. Took me years to get over it. But the Lord was a good husband to me."

I can't imagine the Lord being real enough to someone to be considered a husband. If I had been a religious person and wound up with a violent husband who I had to kill to save my child, I might blame God.

"I guess the reason I told you is to encourage you if you're leaving for the same reason, honey."

She thinks my escape-worthy "situation" was an abusive marriage. I feel a pang of guilt that her compassion for me forced her to confide such a painful story. "I wasn't married," I say, as if that eases it somewhat.

"Good for you. So many girls are desperate and dumb.

They see all the signs, but they marry the man anyway, like I did. Spend the rest of their lives regretting it. No, you're doing the right thing walking away."

I leave it at that. "Thank you."

We stop at a convenience store, and everyone piles in for snacks. There's a Chick-fil-A next door, so I hurry over with half the crowd and get something to eat. I'm not sure where we are. I consider staying here, but I kind of like being with Miss Lucy, so I decide not to get off just yet.

Back on the bus, Miss Lucy shows me pictures of her grandchildren at various ages. She keeps the snapshots in an envelope in her huge purse, and I take them carefully with my fingertips and study them. I love family pictures. Some therapist would probably have a field day with my obsession with them. I'm one of those people who clicks on every photo my friends post on Facebook and Instagram, then I wind up clicking through every shot they have in every album, lingering on pictures of happy families.

Maybe it's because I have sweet memories of my childhood, before everything broke loose.

When I get to the picture of a blonde girl in a homecoming dress, I comment on how pretty she is. Miss Lucy pulls a handkerchief out of her bag, takes her glasses off, and dabs at her eyes. I look up at her, wondering if it's something I've said.

"That's my precious granddaughter, Laura."

"She's beautiful," I say. "How old is she?"

"She's sixteen now. But she went missing a few days after this picture was made."

"Missing? How long ago was that?"

Miss Lucy wipes her eyes. "Two years. The police ruled her a runaway, but we knew better. Something terrible happened to her. She would never have run away like that."

I stare at her picture, trying to imprint it on my brain in case I see her someday.

"She was so excited about the homecoming dance. That picture was taken in the store when she was modeling the dress. Homecoming was going to be her first date a couple of weeks later, and she was over the moon excited. That cameo necklace she's wearing, it used to be mine. I gave it to her to wear with her homecoming dress. It looked so pretty on her. She had all sorts of things coming up that she was looking forward to." She laughs. "Laura doesn't just look forward to things, she bounces like Tigger when she's excited. She was going to sing a solo in an upcoming choir program, and she was thrilled about that. She had been chosen to star in her school play. She'd been rehearsing every day, and she loved every minute of it. No girl with so much going on in her life would just up and leave."

"She looks happy here."

"Not like a runaway." She puts her glasses back on, takes the pictures from me, and gazes down at her again. "We haven't given up. We're still hoping to find her someday."

"What's her last name?" I ask, thinking I'll look up the newspaper articles about her.

"Daly. It was all over the news in Georgia. We had search parties out hunting for her. They dredged the river looking for her. Thank God they never found her . . . that way."

No, her family wouldn't want her to be found dead, even if it brought that overrated word—*closure*. No one wants closure at the expense of their loved one's life.

"The police insisted she'd run away, like that just ended it. My daughter said, 'Well, if you think that's what happened, then find her.' She was fourteen at the time. Where was she? But they finally just gave up on the case, like it was common for a child to hit the road and vanish into thin air. It didn't happen that way, but if it did, what happens to those girls? Where do they go?"

"Police love closing cases," I mutter. "It's an ego thing for some of them."

She packs the pictures back into the envelope and stuffs it into her purse. I wonder how often she takes that picture out. Its corners are worn and bent.

"How are her parents?" I ask.

"Her father, my son-in-law, started drinking heavily and left. They're divorced now. The family has never been the same since. That's one reason I want to go live with them. My daughter needs help. Her other kids are getting short shrift."

I know what that's like. My mother was a wreck after my father's death. She folded into herself and hasn't entirely come out yet.

"How do you get through something like that?" I ask aloud, though I didn't mean to.

"My faith in Jesus," she says.

"Faith?" I ask. "Even when things went so wrong?"

"This is a fallen world, honey," she says.

I look at her. "What does that mean? Fallen?"

She gives me a surprised look, then her face softens. "When Adam and Eve committed that first sin, all hell broke loose. Literally. The curse on humanity from then on was pretty much that we got what we chose. And some people choose evil."

"So God doesn't have control over it?" I ask, hoping I'm not coming across as combative. I just seriously want to know.

"Oh, he has control. But Satan is the prince of this world. Still, he can't do anything without God's permission. The first chapter of Job proves that."

I've never read the book of Job, but I make a mental note to do it when I can. Anything that can help me understand evil could only help.

Though I can't wrap my mind around what Miss Lucy believes, I decide to let it slide. I don't want her to think badly of me.

But she's not finished. It seems important to her to make me understand. "My faith is in Jesus, not in the way human beings behave. And I know this is not all there is. Someday he'll wipe away all my tears."

It sounds nice, but I find it hard to think that way. I'm glad she has something that comforts her, though.

"You don't know Jesus?" she asks me gently.

I've been asked that question a few times in my life, and I confess that it always leaves me stumped. Who can know a man who lived two thousand years ago? I've dwelt on it before, wondering if these Christians sense his presence, if he somehow comes to them like a ghost, offering them smiles and high-fives, comforting them when they grieve, directing them where to find the best parking places.

"No, I can't say that I do."

She isn't appalled. She just pats me on the knee and smiles. "Oh, he would change everything for you."

I bite my tongue. Would he bring her granddaughter back? He hasn't yet. Would he bring my dad back to life? Would he rewind time to the day before Brent was murdered?

My dad's death, now Brent's. These things make up my everything.

We're quiet for a while as we ride, and Miss Lucy leans her head back and falls asleep. Her low snore lulls me to sleep, and I find myself dreaming of her granddaughter in that home-coming dress, standing on a stage singing a solo.

My stomach is sick when I jolt awake. If there's a God, I wonder why he lets good girls go missing and good men die. I wonder how he can stand by as someone who would never have committed murder is blamed for it. Either he's not paying attention, or he doesn't really care.

When we pull over at another Trailways station to let out some passengers and pick up new ones, I get off to use the facilities and buy some food from the vending machine. When I get back on, Miss Lucy is smiling.

"I thought you might get off here. I was hoping you wouldn't."

I shrug. "Guess I'll go to Atlanta."

"You should come two hours farther south to Shady Grove. You'd like it there. Unemployment is zero. The mayor brags that everybody who wants a job there finds one."

I do need to get a job as soon as possible.

"The population is about twenty thousand. Great school system, though you don't have kids. But it's a sweet little town. I think you'd do well there. And your boyfriend isn't likely to find you there. He'd never think of looking for you in Shady Grove."

I tell her I'll think about it. It would be amazing to wind up in a town where I had at least one friend. Miss Lucy could be a source of comfort as the days get darker.

At least until she learns that I'm wanted for murder.

12

DYLAN

There's another guy hitching a ride on the charter flight with me. I'm told he's going to Dallas, but the pilot assures me that Durant will be the first stop since my assignment takes top priority. I assume that means that the Paces paid more for my trip.

The plane is a six-passenger Cessna Citation, a double-engine light jet. I take the backseat because I hope to work on the way, studying the crime scene pictures I snapped on my phone and reading up on Casey Cox. But the Dallas passenger is chatty.

"You fly this way often?" he asks, looking over the back of his seat at me.

I smile. "No, first time. You?"

"All the time. Beats going through security and all the waiting. So I heard them talking about you working on an investigation. You a cop?"

I click off my phone, settling in for the conversation. "I'm a privately contracted investigator. I'm just going to extradite a prisoner." Though it isn't entirely accurate, it seems like a good short answer.

"How long you been a PI?" he asks.

I don't want to tell him I just started today. "I was a 31 Delta in the Army Criminal Investigations Division for the last few years. I was discharged recently. I like the work, so it seemed like a natural fit to be a PI."

"Criminal Investigations? What kind of criminal investigations could there be in the army?"

This could take a while, but I don't really mind. I like to talk about my former career. "Think of 31 Delta as the army's version of the FBI or the Secret Service. We investigate any felony-level crime having to do with army personnel or property."

He sets his arm on the back of the seat and twists more comfortably. "What's the worst case you ever investigated?"

I don't want to say the murder of my best childhood friend, so I come up with another answer. "We had some homicides, some suicides."

"Overseas or stateside?"

"Both."

"So soldiers kill each other?"

"Soldiers are humans in a pressure cooker. If they had criminal or violent tendencies before, they have a way of boiling to the surface when they're in high-stress situations. Yeah, crimes are committed. Criminals are investigated."

"So all those suicides. What do you think causes that?"

I look down, not wanting to meet his eyes. "Those happen mostly stateside after they get home. PTSD, injuries, families who've moved on while they're gone, inability to get jobs . . ." That void in my stomach yawns bigger, and I don't want to talk about it anymore. "So what do you do?"

"I work for a medical equipment manufacturer. Mostly sales."

I try to look interested as he waxes poetic about his work, but as he talks, my mind works through the puzzle of Casey Cox.

⌒

The trip to Durant is much shorter than I expected, and when we land, I'm let off the plane. The pilot tells me that the Paces arranged for a rental car and that the guy monitoring the radio at the fixed-base operator, or FBO, has the keys. I go in and find him sitting behind the counter with the radio mike in front of him. He's gregarious, like a long-lost cowboy friend, and he tosses me the keys.

The car is a shiny black Altima. I sit in it a minute, figuring out where everything is, then I punch the Durant Police Department into my GPS, planning to let them know what I'm doing and enlist their help. I give them pictures of Casey and let them know that she may be connected to a murder in Shreveport. They make a call to Keegan to confirm that I'm legit, then agree to put out an alert on her and tell me they'll help in any way I need.

I'm heading to the store where we know Casey got off the bus when a *boom* shakes the night. I duck, swerve hard off the road, and wind up in a shallow ditch.

When the car stops, I'm sweating and my heart is racing. I can't breathe. I finally force my head up over the dashboard and see a group of kids across the street playing with fireworks.

I wipe my face with shaking hands and tell myself to get a grip. This is ridiculous. There aren't IEDs in Durant, Oklahoma. This is why I was discharged from the army. They said I wasn't functioning well, that my PTSD was severe and disabling.

Maybe they were right. I get out and assess the mess I've gotten myself into. If the ditch had been deeper it would be worse. There doesn't seem to be any damage to the car, but what if I'd been on a four-lane road with traffic on either side?

I get back in and carefully make my way out of the ditch. Thankfully, my wheels don't get stuck, and in just a few minutes I'm back on the road without having to call a tow truck. No one has to know.

I've stopped shaking by the time I get to the convenience store. I go in and show Casey's picture to the night clerk, but he's never seen her. He says he would remember those big eyes, and he's got a particular love of blondes.

I tell him that her hair color and style may have changed, but he's still no help. I stand in front of the store, looking up the street. Casey would have seen a Walgreens about two blocks up. I step to the side of the building and look the other way. Nothing but HUD apartments. I doubt she would have chosen that direction.

I drive up to the twenty-four-hour Walgreens and go in. I head to the nearest clerk and wait in line. The clerk is an elderly lady who should have had the privilege of retiring years ago. She is slow and methodical. I wonder if her back aches, but she smiles and speaks to everyone like a trouper. They should give her a stool or at least offer her the day shift.

When I get up to her, I show her Casey's picture on my phone and ask her if she saw her yesterday.

"I wasn't working yesterday," the woman says. "She doesn't look familiar."

"Is there anyone here who was working yesterday?"

"I think Haley was. She's at the makeup counter." She points, and I see a young woman cleaning the glass counter.

I show Haley the picture. "Can you tell me if you've seen this woman in the last day or so?"

She glances at the picture and starts to say no, but then she frowns and takes the phone out of my hand and moves two fingers out from each other on the screen, enlarging Casey's face. "Why? Are you her boyfriend?"

"No."

"A cop?"

I straighten, certain that she's seen her. "I'm not a cop, but I'm working with the Shreveport Police Department to find her. Someone close to her has died and I need to find her. Did she come in here?"

She pauses for a long moment, studying my face now. I meet her eyes, hoping she'll trust me. "She didn't have hair that length. It was chin length. And she had glasses, but I think it was her. She said her car broke down and she was stranded here for the night."

"Did she buy anything?"

"Yeah, but I don't remember what. She seemed nice. I knocked over an endcap and she thought I was hurt when she saw me on the floor. Oh, wait. I remember. She bought some hair dye. It was dark brown. I noticed because it wasn't the color of her hair."

So by now she's a brunette. Dark brown, chin-length hair, glasses instead of contacts.

"Did you talk?"

"Kind of. Who died? A family member?"

"No, a close friend."

Haley's eyes fill with concern. "She said her phone battery was dead and her car had broken down, so she used our phone to call a cab."

"Did she tell you where she was going?"

"She asked me about the motel up the street, but I told her not to go there. I told her to go to the Hampton Inn, because it's safer."

Perfect.

"Was that yesterday?"

"No, the day before, I think. I was off yesterday."

"What time was it? Do you remember?"

"Probably around four."

I ask her for the number of the cab company Casey took so I can talk to the person who gave her a ride. "Listen, if she happens to come back in, would you call me?" I tear a piece of paper off the notepad I keep in my pocket and write my cell number on it.

"You want me to give her the number?" she asks.

"No," I say quickly. "She won't call."

She stares at me for a moment. "She's in trouble, isn't she?"

I sigh. "Please, will you let me know? It's very important."

She says she will, but I doubt it as I walk out. I can't count on her. But it may not matter. Casey isn't likely to return here, especially if she's in another part of town.

I drive to the Hampton Inn where she was sent and ask to speak to the night manager. I show him my credentials and tell him I need to know if she checked in here.

He lets me see the list of people who checked in between the hours of four and five that evening. There are several women's names, so I jot them all down. "Can you tell me which ones paid with cash?"

He goes deeper into the system, then hands me a name. "Lexi Jones."

Lexi Jones. She must have pulled that out of the air. There's nothing I'm aware of that connects her to that name. "Is she still here?"

He types something into his computer and looks at the checkouts. "No, checked out this morning."

My heart sinks. "Can I see the security video of the time when Lexi Jones checked in?"

The manager calls the Durant police to make sure I have the authority, then he walks me back to the security office and finds that hour. I watch as people come and go, and at about the 4:20 mark, she comes in.

It's Casey for sure—shorter hair and glasses. I put a copy of the video on my thumb drive, print out her picture. "Let me see the video of the time she checked out."

"She did rapid checkout in her room. She wouldn't have come to the desk."

"Still, you may have caught video of her coming through the lobby. I want to see if she changed her appearance again."

He seems caught up in it now, as if loving this new task. We watch for several minutes after she checked out. He clicks it into slow motion each time someone walks through the lobby, then finally we see a brunette hurrying through.

"There," I say. "That may be her."

He stops the playback and enlarges her face. It's grainy, but I can see a girl with brown hair. It's the same glasses, the same duffel bag, the same purse. Yes, that's her. I get him to print a picture and I copy the moment of video to my thumb drive again.

"She hasn't used her phone since she went missing," I say. "Can you tell me if she used her room phone for anything?"

He checks, then shakes his head. "Nope. She didn't."

I think for a moment. She would have wanted to get online, maybe check the news in Shreveport, in order to figure out her next move. "Do you have a business center with computers?"

"Yes, sir, it's downstairs."

He leads me to that room, closed in with glass doors. He swipes his card and opens the door. There are two computers and a printer. I check the browser history on both computers. One person has checked an airline website in the last twenty-four hours. Someone else has checked Amtrak. Just before Amtrak, someone clicked on the newspaper in Shreveport. That must be her. I check the article, see that it's about Brent's death. Yes, she wanted to see if they'd connected her to the murder yet.

Before that, she clicked on a Facebook page. I click on that and see the profile of some guy in Shreveport. I write his name down and see that he had the link to that article. He defends her in his status update. He's clearly a friend of hers.

I go back to the Amtrak page and print that out. If she took a train, she could be anywhere by now. But Amtrak stations do have security. It'll be hard to pick her out of a crowd, but maybe I can find her.

I thank the manager, who's stayed with me the whole time, as if this is his project. He walks taller as we return to the front. I know he'll have a story to tell his family today, especially if Casey is apprehended.

When I get to my car, I send the pictures and videos of her to Keegan in Shreveport, then I call the Durant police and follow up with copies to them. Maybe they'll locate her before I do. I sit in the car for a moment, trying to think like Casey.

There are fast food restaurants within walking distance, but it's late and they're closed. I make a note to come back to them in the morning if I can't locate her through Amtrak. I'll also circle around to the cab service—the only one in town—and find the drivers who took her places. But first I head to the train station, praying she hasn't left town yet.

13

CASEY

By the next morning, when our bus finally pulls into Atlanta after all the stops along the way, I feel I've known Miss Lucy all my life. I don't want to leave her. She's my only friend in this dark new world.

We shuffle off the bus and walk into the terminal, and a cheer goes up as Miss Lucy sees her family—two grandchildren and her daughter—holding a sign that says "Welcome Home, Grandma!" I can't help smiling for her as she bursts into tears and runs to give hugs. I go to the information desk and ask where I can get a cab. But Miss Lucy runs over, takes my arm, and says, "Come over here, hon. I want you to meet my family."

She introduces me to her daughter. There are lines on Sandra's face and the glint of sorrow in her eyes, and I wonder what else her daughter's disappearance has taken from her.

But she's kind to me. "Sounds like you helped take care of Mom on the way here."

I shake my head. "She didn't need any taking care of. She's good company."

"Mom tells me you're getting out of a bad relationship and you're looking for a place to start over. You should really come to Shady Grove. You'd like our little town."

I don't correct her about the bad relationship, and I tell her that I'll think about it. They give me their phone numbers and tell me they'll have me over for dinner if I come. I have to say, I like the thought of that.

I ask the cabdriver to take me to a used car lot in Atlanta. I figure my first order of business should be buying a car. I don't have much to spend, but if I'm lucky, two or three thousand dollars will buy me something halfway reliable. I'm taken to a used car dealership that's open till eight. I find a used Kia with hail damage, but it seems to run well. This model is supposed to get good gas mileage. I do a Carfax check on it and there's no record of it ever being wrecked. I dicker down to three thousand dollars cash. It takes a couple of hours to get the whole thing worked out and get the car detailed—something the dealership insists on—but finally I drive off the lot, feeling freer already.

I head to a drugstore and buy a padded envelope and a temporary phone, then drive to another store ten miles away and buy another phone. I repeat the process with a third store. Once I saw an episode of *24* where they traced a guy based on the consecutive serial numbers on several phones he'd bought at the same time. I don't know if that's even possible, but in case it is, the serial numbers (wherever they are) on mine won't be consecutive. I activate all three with the minutes I bought for each, then sit in the car, staring through the windshield, wondering how I can get one of them to my sister without police intercepting it. It's risky, but I need to talk to her. Eventually it hits me that she goes often to her in-laws' house since her father-in-law is sick with COPD. In fact, once when she was hiding a birthday gift from her husband, she had it sent there. They probably wouldn't think it strange to have something addressed to her delivered there. I address the padded envelope to her, c/o her in-laws. For the return address, I put Jack's Sporting Goods with a fake address in Seattle. I hope they won't notice the postmark.

I write a quick note. "Hannah, don't tell anyone about this. When you're alone, call me on the number in the contact list. Don't do it at home or near your real cell phone. They might be listening."

I take a deep breath, wishing I believed in prayer. It would come in handy now.

I close the package and line up the stamps on it, then drop it in the first mailbox I find. I figure it'll take two or three days to get to her, then maybe another day or so for her to actually receive the package. Any faster way might draw too much attention. I can't wait to talk to her.

My next stop is the Best Buy store at Cumberland Mall. I pick out a small laptop, pay cash again, and walk out with it. I feel like my life is coming back together, though my funds are dwindling.

From there I drive to a hotel way across town from the bus station and check in with my new ID and cash.

14

DYLAN

It's Tuesday morning by the time I talk to the cabdriver who drove Casey from her hotel, and it's clear to me that she went to the Amtrak station yesterday. But after reviewing the camera footage and finding her among the travelers, I see that she got directions from someone who pointed north. So I drive north from the train station and find a Trailways bus station.

There were several buses going out around the time Casey may have been there, but no one at the ticket counter remembers her. The place doesn't have security video. She could have gone north, east, or south. Following any of these buses randomly will be a wild-goose chase.

I finally admit to myself that she's gone and I missed her.

What would I do if I were in her shoes? Since she'd had to leave her computer behind, she would probably want to get a new one. I go to some of the computer stores in Durant, ask if anyone has seen her. I strike out, so I go to the public library. I hit pay dirt right away.

"Yes, she was here the day before yesterday," the librarian on duty tells me. "She was using our computer. I remember her because she stopped a guy from viewing porn in front of a child."

She tells me about the girl who yanked the man's cord and threatened to call his wife. I find that perplexing. Does she compartmentalize her life so that she can murder a guy one day and defend a child's innocence the next? How does that work?

The librarian lets me watch the video footage of that hour in the computer room. I try to figure out what Casey had up on her computer screen, but the picture is grainy. When I check the computer she used, I see the same Facebook page and the Shreveport newspaper again. It tells me nothing about where she's gone.

I don't like defeat, but I finally book my flight home. I need to collect more information about her. There are other ways of figuring out where she went.

Since the charter flight is so expensive and I'm not in a rush, I book a commercial flight home, but I have to drive to Dallas to catch it. I'll return my rental car there.

When I'm almost to the Dallas airport, I call Keegan and give him the bad news.

"How did she get past you?" he asks, clearly ticked off.

"She didn't get past me," I say, aware that I sound defensive. "She had already left by the time I got here. She's smart. She's staying off the grid and covering all her bases. She changed hotels, paid with cash, didn't talk to many people."

"She's a twenty-five-year-old girl who has never plotted out a crime before. How would she know how to stay so far under the radar?"

"Her dad was a cop, right? Maybe she picked up some things from him. Or maybe she reads a lot."

Keegan doesn't like my explanations. "Just come home, and we'll take it from here."

I don't say it, but I have no intention of disappointing the Paces. I hang up and pull my car into the rental return lane. I've cut it close, and I get to the terminal just in time to board. On the flight home, I try to regroup. First I'll talk to the Paces, make sure they want me to continue. If they do, I'll go visit Casey's mother and sister. I'll talk to her friends. I'll find out what Brent had been like lately, what mood Casey had been in. What was on her computer at work.

I'll keep on with the investigation and find this girl who killed my friend. She won't get away with it on my watch.

"We want you to keep looking, Dylan." Jim Pace's voice is raspy and hoarse the next morning. Elise has never looked worse, and I wonder if she's eating and sleeping.

"Police Chief Gates is our friend," Elise says, "and even he has admitted that he doesn't have the manpower to find her. You're our best hope."

Keegan doesn't like it, but with the police chief bending over backward to help the Paces, he doesn't have much choice. They all agree I'll stay on the case.

As soon as I've gotten the all clear, I go to Casey's mother's house. There are members of the media on the street out front, cameramen armed with their equipment. I pull into the driveway.

When I get out, two reporters yell out at me. "Who are you?"

"Nobody," I say as I walk to the door. The reporters have to stay back at the street or risk charges of trespassing.

At first, no one answers the door, and I feel self-conscious standing there, knowing the bloodhounds are watching. If Mrs. Cox is home, she probably thinks I'm another reporter.

"Mrs. Cox," I say through the door. "I'm an investigator working with the Shreveport police. I need to talk to you."

I hear the dead bolt turning once, twice . . . four times before the door opens. The house inside is dark, but I see a few inches' width of a small woman. "I've already talked to police," she says, then she silently mouths the words she just spoke.

I try to look unthreatening. In jeans and a plain gray T-shirt, I hope I do. I hold up my credentials. "I know, but I have a few more questions. Can I come in for a minute?"

She hesitates.

"I just don't want any of this overheard," I whisper, gesturing to the reporters. "No need to give them more than they've got already."

She considers that, then opens the door a little wider. It isn't until I step inside that I realize she couldn't open it any wider because there's junk stacked behind the door.

"I'm sorry for the mess," she says. "I was just cleaning up."

I look around at the ceiling-high mound of stuff and doubt that's true. This place would take weeks to clean out. She points me to one of the only pieces of furniture not covered with her hoard. It's a recliner. As I sit, she pulls a folding chair out of a stack, then digs for a second one, which she sets up next to it.

"I'm sorry," I say, getting back up. "Did you want me to sit there?"

"No," she says. "You're fine there. I just like even numbers." She mouths that last sentence again, then looks at a digital clock on the table, next to six more that aren't powered on. Her eyes linger on the numbers.

Maybe she has an appointment. "Mrs. Cox, I won't keep you long."

I make out a couch under all the debris, but it's stacked three feet high with boxes. On the boxes I see pictures of blenders and Crock-Pots. I also notice a stack of new clothes with price tags and an open rubber bin containing flowerpots. There are at least two of every color.

"I'm sorry for the mess," she says again. "I was just cleaning."

OCD, I think. Mrs. Cox has a bad case of obsessive-compulsive disorder. She's a small, attractive woman who doesn't look like the type to live in a nightmare like this. She's wearing floral capri pants and a pullover blouse, lime green. She's around fifty and looks like one of those women who tries, not like those who've given up at her age. She has makeup on and has done her hair, but her eyes are bloodshot and red, and there are dark circles under them. I can see that her daughter's troubles are taking their toll on her, and she already had problems.

"Casey didn't do it," she says suddenly. "You don't know her. Ask any of her friends, anybody who's ever known her. She's a good and compassionate girl. She would never hurt anyone, least of all Brent." As she silently repeats that, she turns to the clock again. I look at the readout. I've investigated people with OCD before, and they often get fixated on numbers. She might be adding them up in her head, checking for odd numbers, or something like that.

"Do you have any theories about what happened?" I ask in a gentle voice, trying to distract her. "Why she would run away if she's innocent?"

Casey's mother turns from the clock. She gets up and touches a picture of Casey, dusts it with a swipe of her hand, touches it again twice. "You have to understand Casey. When she was twelve . . ." Her voice trails off.

"I know about your husband's death," I say, not wanting to make her say it.

She stands and picks up the stack of clothes, moves it to the other side of the room, as if that's where it belongs. "Whatever they told you, my husband didn't kill himself. He was murdered. Casey knew it, and we all knew it."

I frown, wondering what I've missed. "But the coroner's report, the autopsy, the police findings . . . they all point to suicide."

She sits back down. "Of course they do. But those are lies. If you're a good cop, then examine the evidence. Don't just accept the report."

"I'm not a cop," I say as she mouths. "I'm a private investigator consulting with the police department."

She sighs. "Of course. If you were a cop, you wouldn't be asking questions about Andy."

I think for a moment about what she said. Her husband was a cop. She must know the culture. "So what do you think your husband's death has to do with Casey leaving? Are you saying she was traumatized? Disturbed? Did the event cause depression in her? Anxiety?"

Her mother's eyes brim with tears. "Everything has everything to do with everything."

The phrase takes me aback. "I'm sorry, but I don't understand."

Her face takes on an empty, haunted look, but she keeps talking. "Casey was traumatized." She gets up and touches each box on her couch. "She was never the same. Oh, there were parts of her that were. Her personality couldn't be quashed. But there were times when you could see the ghost in her eyes."

She picks at the tape on the blender box and opens it. "I should've helped her more. She was so young. There were days when I thought it was a suicide and I was so mad at Andy that I couldn't think. But it never made sense."

"Suicide never does," I say.

"It wasn't suicide," she repeats. "Those thoughts came in my weakest days, when I just wanted it all to end." She turns to me now, checking her face with her fingertips. "I have OCD, Detective."

I don't tell her I know.

"I kept picturing his hanging himself over and over, trying to work it out in my head, but Casey kept saying there was blood . . ."

I can't imagine what this woman has been through. "Is that when your OCD started?"

"No," she says. "I had things before . . . rituals, they call them . . . but they weren't . . . disruptive. It got worse after Andy died." Her lips move again.

I picture her dealing with that madness while her daughter needed help herself.

"Casey kept telling me that the police covered things up, that the newspapers had the wrong information, that he was murdered. No one listened to her. I didn't listen. She was just a traumatized kid and that scene kept playing in my mind like it really happened. For so long I didn't listen."

"Do you think Brent's death had anything to do with Andy's death?"

She grows very still for a minute. "Maybe, but not the way you think. Casey must have found Brent, but she didn't kill him."

"Did she tell you that?"

"No," she says, then repeats it with her lips. "I haven't seen my daughter in over a week. Haven't talked to her either. I'd give anything for a phone call. To know she's all right."

I can see by the glisten in her eyes that she means it. Maybe I shouldn't, but I believe her. "Brent was a childhood friend of mine. We met in kindergarten and grew up together."

Her face twists as tears escape her eyes. She pulls two tissues out of a box and wipes her eyes. "I'm so sorry. It's your loss too."

I swallow. "I hadn't seen him in a couple of years, since my deployment with the army. What was their relationship like?"

She sniffs hard. "They were close friends, she said. But I think he was in love with her. Casey had a hard time letting people get close to her. I mean, she has all these close friends, but I don't remember her ever letting anything go beyond friendship with a guy."

"She's twenty-five. Why do you think that is?"

"She's broken." The words are hard for her. "You wouldn't know it. She doesn't seem broken, but she is. I think Brent knew it. He cared about her. I could see it."

I think about the Brent I knew. Though girls always gravitated to him, he was generally slow to make his move. Still, I can't picture him as a puppy dog, following a girl who ultimately murdered him. He wasn't stupid like that.

"Do you know if she's all right?" she asks. "If she's even alive?"

The question surprises me. "Yes, we've been tracking her. She was most recently in Durant, Oklahoma, but she seems to be on the move again."

"Why would she go there? We don't have any family there. None at all. What is she thinking?"

"That's what I was hoping you could tell me."

She shakes her head. "Casey's the smartest girl I know. She thinks things through. Whatever she's doing, she has a good reason."

I ask her if I can see the room where Casey grew up. She takes me down a five-foot-wide passage through the kitchen. More stuff, piled above her head. The things are duplicates of each other stacked in even numbers, grouped according to likeness. Despite the hoarding, the house smells clean.

When we reach Casey's childhood room, I see that it's another storage area. The room is painted lavender, and there are colorful handmade flowers, faded now—three feet wide, at least—hanging on the walls. There are family pictures on her walls from before her dad died. He's in every one. The house looks uncluttered in the pictures. So the hoarding started after his death too.

A phrase from high school physics pops into my head. *For every action, there's an equal and opposite reaction.* The vacuum in Mrs. Cox's life from her husband's death resulted in her hoarding stuff to try to fill that hole. The death in Casey's past may have led to another death.

I leave without any new clues, but I know Casey a little better than I did.

15

CASEY

My sister's call comes Thursday, two days after I sent her the phone. It scares me to death when it rings. I fumble to answer it.

"Hello?"

"Casey, I'm so glad to hear your voice," Hannah blurts. "Are you all right?"

"Yeah, I'm fine. Did your in-laws ask questions about the package?"

"No, I recognized your handwriting. I told them it was something I ordered for Jeff."

"You're not at home or in your car, are you? The police could be listening."

"No, I'm walking at the park. Casey, what happened with Brent?"

I sigh. "They got to him. He had proof about Dad's murder, and they found out." My voice catches. "If he hadn't been digging to help me, he'd be alive."

"You found his body?"

"Yes. He told me to come over on my lunch hour and see what he'd dug up. When I got there . . ." My voice trails off. "I panicked. Just knew I'd have to leave town, that everything was about to go wrong and nobody would listen."

"Casey, listen to me," Hannah says. "Brent sent you a package."

I'm silent for a moment as my mind races back to my phone conversation with him that morning. "Yeah, he told me he did, that he sent me his evidence just as a backup in case anything went wrong. But I figured they'd intercepted that already."

"They didn't. I tried going to your apartment, but it was sealed. Then your landlord came out and handed me the package. I guess it didn't occur to him to give it to the police. He said, 'If you talk to Casey, tell her I'm praying for her. I know she didn't do what they're saying.'"

Tears come to my eyes. Good old Mr. Criswell. I love that man. "What's in it?" I ask.

"It's a thumb drive. It must have the evidence."

"I need it," I tell her.

"I could see what's on it and e-mail the files to you."

"No, I don't want the files on your computer. It's dangerous. I want you playing dumb so they don't see you as a threat. You don't even need to see those files. Can you just FedEx it to me here?"

She says she will, and I get a catch in my stomach before giving her my hotel address. I don't want to stay here this long, but at some point I'm going to have to risk it. This is important. "Send it to my hotel under the name of Grace Newland. But don't try to reach me here after that. I'll leave the minute I get the package tomorrow."

"How will I pay for it? Don't I need a credit card or something? Won't they be watching my accounts?"

"Don't use your real name. Pay cash."

"What if they're watching me and follow me to the FedEx place?"

I think about that for a moment. I don't want my sister getting into trouble, being labeled an accessory to murder. "I don't know. Maybe it's too risky."

"I have an idea," she says. Her voice bumps with each step. "I'll send your package under a fake name, but I'll FedEx something to my friend Liz in New York at the same time. Then if they follow me there and they check to see what I was shipping, they'll find that."

I try to imagine that scenario. Hannah getting out of her car at FedEx with one package in her hand and another one tucked in her bag. She goes in, mails both things with cash.

Cops go in, ask what Hannah Boon shipped, and they find the one thing with her name and return address on it.

"What if the clerk remembers that you shipped two packages?"

"The clerks at FedEx are always busy," she says. "It'll be okay. You have to see what's on this drive so you can prove who really killed Brent."

"And Dad. Listen, Hannah. If anyone drags up Dad's case and asks you about it, you keep telling them you agree with police that it was a suicide. As long as they think you've bought into that, you won't be a threat to them."

"But what about Mom?"

"I don't think she threatens them. They can just write her off as being mentally ill. Besides, if I told her not to say something, she'd have no choice but to say it over and over."

"Casey, I'm scared for you."

I don't tell her I'm scared too. "How *is* Mom?"

"Petrified. She's been crying since you left, repeating her rituals over and over. She went shopping, bought a carload of stuff, from cat litter to all these broken lamps at some thrift store that she claims she's gonna fix."

"All in pairs?"

"Of course. Soon she won't even have a path to her bedroom."

"Is she taking her meds?"

"I think so. I'm trying to get her to go to her shrink and get them adjusted, but you know how she is."

"Tell her I'm fine," I say. "I'll land on my feet. That's what we do in this family, right?"

Hannah's voice is weak. "Sometimes."

"Tell her this will all be sorted out as soon as I figure out a way through it. The system is still as messed up as it was when Dad died. I can't trust it."

"Casey, Brent's family hired a private investigator to look for you. He talked to Mom."

I squeeze my eyes shut. "How can they think I did this? I know they didn't know me well, but they should trust Brent's judgment in friends."

I can hear her sniffing. Her voice grows more distant. "I gave the press an old picture of you. You don't look like that anymore."

"I know, I saw that. Thank you."

"Where will you go?" she asks.

"It's better if you don't know," I say.

"Do I need to destroy this phone?"

I wish I knew more about how they work. "It's probably okay for now. Just keep it hidden. I won't call you, but I might text. Keep it silenced."

My big sister is smart. I know she'll do what I say. "I love you, sis. Please be careful."

I hold the line for a moment too long, then tell her I love her, too, and hang up. I stare at the phone, then take out the battery, drop the phone on the floor, and smash it under my heel.

My connection to my life is broken again.

The package from my sister arrives at my Atlanta hotel at nine thirty the next morning. I already have my car loaded, and I sit in the driver's seat waiting for the FedEx truck. The moment the truck drives away, I go in and retrieve my package, addressed to Grace Newland.

After checking out, I go to the nearest mall and sit in the parking lot. I fire up my computer, then plug in the thumb drive. There's only one folder.

When I open it, I see a list of files. I click on one that says "Cox Case File." Up come pages of documents that Brent scanned into his computer. Somehow he'd gotten the entire file on my father's death, the evidence logged at the scene after I found him, my own written and video testimony, the autopsy report, then the sudden declaration that it was a suicide, the end of the investigation. I go back to the list of files, see a video marked "Sara Meadows." I don't know who that is, so I click on the file.

"This is Brent Pace," my friend says off-camera. My hand comes up to my mouth at the sound of his voice, pain twisting in my throat. "I'm interviewing Sara Meadows, employed with the Shreveport Police Department. She was a clerk in the evidence room at the time of Andrew Cox's death and still works there. Ms. Meadows, you said you were good friends with Officer Cox in the years leading up to his death."

"Yes," she says in a weak voice. "He was a good man. A

very good man. He loved his family and his daughters, and he would never have killed himself. Never. It was all a lie."

"Do you know why it was ruled suicide?"

"I think the investigators were covering up," she says. "I've lived with this for thirteen years, kept my mouth shut, but it's not right. I have stage-four cancer now, and I want to tell what I know."

"What do you want us to know?" Brent asks gently.

"That Officer Cox had evidence that several of the detectives on the force were taking bribes and extorting money from people. People I would call mafia, though when I said that to him, he said that I'd read too many books. It was a kind of organized crime that extorted money from businesses and harassed people into paying. There were some deaths when people fought back, and the findings of those homicides weren't consistent with the evidence logged. Andy was looking in to some of the things these guys had bought with the money, paid cash for, and put under different names so they wouldn't be caught. After a couple of weeks, he came back to me, really shaken at what he'd found. Within three weeks, he was dead."

I can't believe Brent got this interview. No wonder he was so excited when he called me that morning. He must have just talked to her. "So you think he was murdered to keep him from reporting that?"

"What do you think?"

Brent pauses. "Did you tell anyone at the police department?"

I hold my breath during a long pause, then finally she says,

"No, I was afraid. I thought they'd kill me too. But I made note of the evidence that came in, the stuff that was disregarded, like blood evidence from unidentified people. After the CSIs logged the evidence, the lead investigators determined what was relevant. The rest was pushed aside. It always worked out that they were the ones investigating these deaths. After Andy's death, the CSIs logged pictures of Andy's hands with injuries, indicating that he'd struggled, that there was an altercation. Those blood samples need to be compared to those detectives who worked that case. But all that was covered up."

I feel the blood rush from my face. I told them, over and over . . .

My father's dead image flashes into my mind. The rope around his neck, the way his body swayed when I touched it . . . the blood under his fingernails, on his hands . . . the smear on the carpet.

I'd told them he must have been fighting someone, that he had scratches on his arms, that his lip was busted. But that was never mentioned in the media. It just went away, like I'd never said it. But I know what I saw.

"Why would they have logged that as evidence if they were trying to cover it up?" Brent asks.

"I think most of the CSIs are good guys," Sara says. "They did their jobs. I'm sure the killers had cleaned up the scenes as much as they could, but they couldn't hide everything. If the CSIs logged something that implicated the detectives, they just quashed it."

"My friend Casey Cox is the one who found her father dead," Brent says. "She never thought it was a suicide."

"I know!" the woman says, and veins protrude on her temple. "It was horrible, them leaving him for his daughter to find. You'd have to be a sociopath to do that. To traumatize that girl that way. Andy adored her. He never would have let that happen. He was found hanging from the fan in his living room. He would have known Casey would be the next one home."

I wipe away a tear that has found its way to my cheek, then clasp my hands to still them.

"So you don't think the CSIs are involved?" Brent asks.

"I didn't until one of them was killed in a single-vehicle accident . . . just out of the blue. Other one retired and left the state."

"So let me get this straight," Brent says. "The detectives who covered up . . ."

"The only ones I know for sure are Gordon Keegan and Sy Rollins."

I cover my face, so grateful that someone has uttered the unspeakable.

"Were you able to keep any of the evidence?" Brent asks her.

"The whole case file. I've hidden it all these years. I made a copy for you."

When the recording ends, I close it and go back to the documents. I click on the evidence list. My stomach churns as I review what they took from my house.

The list is incomplete. Dad's laptop was removed, but it's not shown here. The file box in Dad's office at home was taken, and it doesn't appear on the list. His car was searched, which doesn't even make sense if they thought it was a suicide, but none of that shows up on the list.

I go back to the autopsy report, which my mother never let me see when I was twelve. I study it, trying to make sense of the medical lingo. Brent has highlighted one statement. "Bleeding on brain consistent with blunt head trauma, though primary cause of death was asphyxiation from hanging."

In the margin of this report is Brent's handwriting: "Wouldn't that indicate that there was an altercation before he was hanged?"

I frown and read on. The medical examiner drew no conclusion about that. I wonder why not. Wouldn't that be obvious to anyone with a scalpel?

I remember seeing the blood in various places around the room. A smudge on the carpet, a dragged fingerprint on the wall . . . They'd been wiped clean the next time I went into the house.

Next in the stack of documents is a list of possessions Gordon Keegan has been seen using during his time off. A sailboat, a motorcycle, an RV that probably cost over $100,000, all owned by a company named MNO Enterprises. Brent includes pictures of Keegan using them like they're his. He's taken his family and his brother's family on annual trips to Hawaii—Brent has pictures from Keegan's niece's Facebook page—and has also gone to Europe several times. My dad was never able to do or buy those things on a cop's salary. I wonder how the department never realized this.

The other cops involved have lists of toys and trips, too, also owned by MNO. Brent didn't leave it at that. He tracked down MNO Enterprises. It's owned by a company called Tidewater Realty in Grand Cayman. Classic money laundering. Brent did a lot of snooping around. Leave it to a journalist to have the kind of curiosity that would lead to his death.

I feel sick that he did this for me. Yes, he was sniffing for a great story he could break, but mostly he knew that the whole thing ate me from the inside out. He wanted me to have resolution. But word must have gotten to Keegan and Rollins that he was digging around.

Now they've gotten him too.

Thoughts of Brent's crime scene nauseate me more. When I found Brent, I didn't look for his computer or the documents he said he was going to give me that day. I just felt for a pulse, did CPR, tried to rouse him. But his body was already cold. When I finally realized he was gone, I stumbled out, numb from shock and fear.

In case there's a God, I thank him for giving Brent the wisdom to put a flash drive in the mail to me before he saw me, just in case anything happened. He knew what he was dealing with.

I sit in my car and weep as time ticks by. There's nothing I can do about all this. I don't know who at the police department is clean. This evidence could acquit me, or it could lead to my death. And if I die, they'll keep getting away with it. More will die, and more will be traumatized and abused.

Somehow I have to expose them, but if I get caught, they'll confiscate all my evidence and destroy it. And they'll get away with it anyway.

I'm not brave. I don't want to go to jail for something I didn't do. Worse, I don't want to be murdered like Brent and my father. I don't want my family butchered to make a statement. Mom, Hannah, my sweet little Emma.

I have to stay hidden for now. I look on Google Maps and see the towns north of Atlanta, west, south. Part of me longs to go where Miss Lucy lives. I need friends, and she makes me feel anchored somehow.

There's no reason for anyone to look for me in Shady Grove, and that's as good a reason to go there as any. I type in the town and get the directions, then pull back onto the road.

As I drive out of town, I wipe the tears from my face. "Daddy and Brent," I whisper. "I'm going to prove what happened to you. I just need a little more strength." But they can't hear me, and anything they had the power to give me is already mine. They can't give me anything more.

The grave has never seemed more final.

I wish I could believe in the afterlife.

16

CASEY

As soon as I get to Shady Grove, I see a motel on Main Street called Gran's Porch Motel. The rooms look like little white cottages, and there's a courtyard at the center that has what looks like a porch. Something about it draws me, so I check in there. I like the idea of saying I have to go to Gran's Porch rather than "the motel."

I picture a family opening this place for travelers on their way down to Florida, hoping to offer homelike comfort. But the man behind the desk doesn't seem to care much. He's smoking a cigar that makes me cough, but he takes my cash for a week's stay and gives me the key card.

The place is clean, and the room has everything I need. A bed, a chair, a kitchenette. I'll be okay here until I find an apartment.

Leaving my car in the parking lot, I walk up the strip of adjacent stores and offices, looking for a Help Wanted sign. I'll take anything. Just something to earn a living so that I can pay back my nest egg and get by day-to-day. I stop at two restaurants, tell them I've just moved here, ask them if they have any openings. Neither one does, but I leave an application just in case, under the name of Grace Newland.

I like Shady Grove. Its name makes sense, given all the trees that shade the roads. Whoever planned this town had a special respect for trees. It makes me feel warm, at home, and—except for the motel manager—the town and people have a Mayberry feel that makes me think I could actually make it here if I have to stay forever.

I finally see a Help Wanted sign in the window of a store called Simmons Cell Repair. I don't know anything about servicing cell phones, but I decide to try it anyway. I push through the glass door, wait for a man who's talking to a customer. I browse the glass cases until he's ready for me, and finally, he turns. "Help you, ma'am?"

I smile at him. "Hi, I'm Case—" I stop midword and correct myself. "Grace Newland. I just moved to the area and saw the Help Wanted sign on the door."

He tells me his name—Stan Simmons—and looks me over. "Do you have any experience working with cell phones?"

"No, but I'm a quick learner. Anything you teach me I can pick up right away. If there are manuals, I can read them all tonight. Most of my experience is office work."

"So what brings you to Shady Grove?" he asks.

"I just like this town. I thought it would be a nice place to live."

He gives me a questioning look, and I'm sure he's going to dig for more, but he doesn't. "Yeah, it is a good town. When I was in high school I had every intention of moving to a big city. Spent two years in Chicago but couldn't wait to get back. You seem like a smart lady." He inclines his head and studies me. "Can I count on you staying awhile? You're not going to get homesick and take off back home next week, are you?"

"No," I say. "I'm staying."

He looks hard into my eyes, as if assessing me for truth, and sweat prickles my underarms. "I'm not expecting somebody to fix the phones," he says. "My techs and I do that. But we also sell refurbished phones, and you would have to help do that. You'd mostly be a sales clerk, taking down what's wrong with the phones people bring in for service, calling people when they're ready, that kind of thing. You need to be good with people."

I give him my best smile again. "I think I can be. My mama taught me good manners."

He smiles. "We have five other employees, but one just had a baby, two of them are techs who do the repairs, and two of them are in college. We need somebody full time."

"I can work full time," I say, "and I can start right away."

"One other thing," he says. "This is a subcontracting job. In other words, I can't afford to offer you health insurance or match your social security. So all my employees are subcontracted."

I think about that for a moment, wondering if this is a trap. To the IRS, I'll be self-employed. I'll have to pay my taxes and social security myself. He won't withhold anything from my checks.

It actually might be a blessing in disguise. A way to stay off the grid, at least until taxes are due next April. "I guess that's okay," I say. "When can I start?"

"Monday?" he asks.

It's Friday now, so that will give me the weekend to get settled in. "Sure, no problem."

He reaches out a hand and we shake. "Let me get you to fill out some paperwork so I can get all your info. You're hired as far as I'm concerned."

I wonder if he is the *only* one concerned, but I quickly fill out the application with everything I know about Grace Newland. Then I turn it in, feeling a little sad that I've had to deceive him. I'm getting tired of the lies, but what can I do?

I notice the cross on the wall and a framed Scripture verse. "Come to Me, all who are weary and heavy-laden, and I will give you rest." Though I'm not a believer, I've had good experiences with people who are. They're usually nice people trying to do the right thing. I'm always baffled by the way the media portrays them. If I'd never met one, I'd think they were all mean, intolerant prudes who wanted the world to line up like robots. I'm sure there are some who are shrill and bitter, but for the true believers—the ones comfortable talking about their faith, like Miss Lucy—I've only been left with good feelings. I like people who stand up for their convictions, even if I don't share them.

I think I'll be fine working for Mr. Simmons. I turn the application back in, and he looks it over, then says, "See you Monday! We open at ten, but I need you to be here at nine."

I have a little jaunt to my step as I head back to the motel. I'm making progress. Once I feel like the earth has stopped trembling beneath my feet, then I can worry about proving my innocence and exposing the ones who murdered Brent and my father. But for now, I just have to stay hidden from day-to-day and forge what little life I can.

17

_____

CASEY

When I get back to Gran's Porch, I sit in the quiet of my room and count out my money. I spent $3,000 on the car, plus taxes, then $600 on the laptop. I laid down $400 on bus tickets and $600 on hotel bills. I've also bought food and telephones and paid for the driver's license and social security card, taxis, and a few incidentals I've needed along the way. I figure I've already spent $6,500, and counting out my remaining cash confirms that. Only $5,500 left. Somehow I have to replenish it. I can't keep spending like this.

I realize that I didn't ask my new boss what he would pay

me, but even if it's minimum wage, at least it's something. Sighing, I use the phone I've designated as my Shady Grove phone and call Miss Lucy at the number she gave me. She answers quickly.

"Hello?" Her voice sounds happy and upbeat.

"Miss Lucy? This is Grace."

I can hear the smile in her voice. "Grace, it's so good to hear from you. Are you still in Atlanta?"

"No, ma'am," I say. "I decided to come to Shady Grove. You put a hard sell on me. It sounded like a good place."

"Oh, I'm so happy," she says. "Now I have exactly one friend in town! You have to stay here with me. You can sleep in my bed and I'll sleep on the couch."

I would never make Miss Lucy sleep on the couch! "No, ma'am, I can't do that. I'm doing fine. I even got a job already."

"Where, dear?" she asks me.

"Simmons Cell Repair on Main Street. They had a Help Wanted sign, so I went in. They hired me on the spot. I start Monday."

Miss Lucy's pride beams in her voice. "You have a way about you, sweetheart. Now, you have to come over for dinner to celebrate."

"No," I say. "You just got there. I can't make more work for Sandra."

"But I'm cooking. Sandra loves having company. Now, you come at six, and here's the address. Got a pen?"

Miss Lucy won't take no for an answer, and frankly, I

would really like to see her again. I finally agree and write down the address.

But her invitation to stay at their house is totally out of the question. I can't make her guilty of harboring a criminal or being an accessory to murder. She doesn't know who I am, but one day she might find out, and if she believes their story, it could break her heart. I can't stand that thought.

But just eating with them shouldn't implicate them. It would be good to be among friends tonight—even brand-new friends who know nothing true about me.

⌁

I show up at their house with a pot of flowers I picked up at Kroger, and they all seem glad to see me. We eat roast beef with potatoes and carrots smothered with gravy. I try not to eat too much, but it's been a while since I've had a home-cooked meal. After dinner, Sandra's kids clean the dishes, and Miss Lucy takes me into the missing girl's room on the third floor, a room converted from attic space.

"Sandra has kept Laura's room just like it was when she left it," Miss Lucy says. "She didn't make up her bed that day, so it's still like that." Her eyes tear up as she points to the shoes lying on their sides where Laura had kicked them off the day of her disappearance. "Coming in here makes me feel like she's still with us, like she'll walk back in any minute."

"Have the police got any leads?" I ask in a quiet voice, feeling strangely like I'm standing on sacred floorboards.

"No, none. They combed the woods and dredged the lakes, offered rewards, but finally, when they couldn't solve the case, I think they just gave up. They ruled her a runaway. But look." She points to the girl's computer table, where tickets to an Alicia Keys concert sit. "Sandra says Laura was so excited about getting those tickets that she practically had to peel her off the ceiling. She couldn't wait for it. And this." She points to a math notebook open on the bed. "She did her math homework the very day she disappeared. Why would a girl go to the trouble of doing her homework if she knew she was running away? No, something happened to her."

I'm quiet as I look at the pictures of Laura around the room, all in groups with her friends. I don't touch anything, but I bend over and study her features. "She's really pretty."

"She's out there somewhere," Lucy says. "We have prayed and prayed that wherever it is, God would show her an escape."

I look back at her. "There was Elizabeth Smart. She was found. And those three girls in Ohio."

"Yeah, that's what we keep thinking. It could happen for her. But what has she been through in the meantime?"

I wonder how Miss Lucy feels about her prayers not being answered, and why she keeps believing when things have gone so terribly wrong.

It's almost like she reads my mind. "The Lord sometimes

uses sorrow in our lives to deepen us," Miss Lucy says. "This is one of those times."

"Why do we have to be deep?" I wonder aloud.

Miss Lucy looks at me as if she's never considered that question. "Because what good are we if we're shallow? He can use us when we have some depth. He had sorrows, so why shouldn't we?"

I give her a soft smile. "You're a very understanding soul."

"Because I don't blame God? Well, it's true. He did have sorrows. Betrayal, abuse, heartbreak, physical beatings, the worst death imaginable."

I don't say so, but I don't understand why that had to happen. Christians always act like Jesus' death on a cross was inevitable, like Jesus *had* to die the way he did. But I don't see it. For instance, why did God set such a high price on sin? Hadn't he ever heard of a discount? Couldn't he have accepted all those bulls and goats being sacrificed and called it even?

"I sometimes think that if there's a God, he's too hard on us," I admit.

Miss Lucy sits down on Laura's bed, runs her hand along the sheets. "Were your parents hard on you when you were a child?" she asks.

I didn't expect that question. I think back. "My dad was, but not my mom. She had some struggles of her own, so she was pretty easy to get around. But Dad . . . he was the one who could be stern with us. But he also showed us that he was our biggest fan."

IF I RUN

"He sounds like a good man."

"Yeah, he was."

"Was?"

I swallow the knot in my throat. "He died when I was twelve."

"I'm sorry, sweetheart." She takes my hand, pats it. "Well, that's how God is with us. He teaches us hard things, sometimes has to be stern with us, and disciplines us. All because he loves us."

"Do you think that's why Laura disappeared? Because you were being *disciplined*?"

"No!" she says without hesitation. "Evil just exists in the world. It will be repaid, but not yet. The devil gets his way sometimes, but it won't last. Jesus said that the prince of this world now stands condemned. His time is short."

I know the devil. His name is Gordon Keegan, and he's on the Shreveport Police Department. He got his way in my father's and Brent's deaths. He's trying to get his way with me.

If there is a God, I don't see any evidence that he's got Keegan in his crosshairs.

Her words hang in my head as we go downstairs. I look at the other pictures of Laura framed and hanging on the walls among her siblings. I've been trying to imagine what might have happened to her, so finally, I ask. "What exactly happened the day Laura disappeared? Where was she?"

"She was at a bonfire on the lake with her youth group that night. Her friends saw her there. One of them said she went to the porta-potty, and she just never came back."

135

"That's awful," I say. "How long before they realized she was missing?"

"Probably a couple of hours of her not answering texts or phone calls and never coming back. There were about fifty kids there, and I imagine everyone thought she was with someone else. The youth minister finally called Sandra to see if she'd gone home. That's when we called the police. At first they didn't take it seriously. They figured she'd gotten a ride with a boy or something, that she'd be back."

"Did she have a boyfriend?"

"No. There was a guy she liked at the time," Miss Lucy says, "but he wasn't reciprocating. Her friends said he'd spent some time talking to her that night, though, and she was very excited. But he was at the bonfire the whole night. Her friends say there's no way she would have just left the party without telling anybody."

There's movement in the kitchen doorway, and I see Sandra standing there. I wonder if we should shut up, if this conversation will upset her. But she comes in and pulls out a chair. "Some of the youth group said they'd seen a dirty blue van with Kentucky plates parked near the rest of the cars," she says. "They'd joked about whose car it was. It was gone when they started looking for her. But if that was the person who took her, no one else saw him, and that van was never seen again. She could be anywhere."

The mood stays somber as I help finish cleaning the kitchen, so I finally thank them for their hospitality and tell them I need to get home to bone up on what I'll be selling at my new job.

As I drive to my room, I think about the hole left in that family, the hole that will never be filled as long as Laura is missing. It's so like the hole in my own family, the one that keeps sucking others into its vortex.

I wonder if the ones left behind should even be called survivors. We're like half-dead souls, circling the vortex, waiting to get sucked in too.

18

DYLAN

Facebook is the pot of gold at the end of an investigator's rainbow, and I take advantage of it now, checking the profile, pictures, and videos of every person Casey has ever friended. I work out a timeline of parties she's attended, outings with her friends, dinners in restaurants. Even Brent's page is full of information. Casey is in at least half the pictures he's posted in the last year.

I find one of her friends who posts from the moment she wakes up until she goes to bed at night. I don't know her, but I have friends like her, friends who miss their lives as they stay glued to their phones, letting everyone know of every thought they have and every bite they eat. I wonder if this girl ever interacts much with real friends—people who are truly present in her life. She probably never enjoys a meal because she's too busy posting pictures of it. Too busy to enjoy her friends' quips because she's thumb-typing every word.

I find a ton of information about Casey, studying the pictures and the videos this girl named Brittany has posted. Casey's not an attention hog. She's friendly in most of the videos, usually listening intently with interest in her eyes as one of her friends drones on. In some of the videos, I see Casey in the background, washing dishes and cleaning up after they've eaten. She's always the one being useful.

In one of the clips, her friends are giggling hysterically after drinking too much, and someone says, "Casey's the only one here with her head on straight."

Casey just smiles.

"She didn't drink anything tonight," the person with the camera says. "Casey, what is wrong with you? Why can't you drink with us?"

I find myself grinning with her smirk as she answers. "Have you seen yourself drunk?"

"So what are you saying? You don't want to be like me?"

"I don't need to have a buzz to have fun with you guys."

"She *is* saying she doesn't want to be like you, Brit," one of the guys says. "You're a stupid drunk."

"And you're not?" Brittany says in a huff.

"No. I'm a cerebral drunk."

Another person who looks ragged speaks up. "They say that whatever you are in your real personality, you just become more of it when you drink. So like, if Brittany's a stupid drunk, that means she's always stupid. Drinking is just stupid on steroids. Rick is naturally smart, so he's a smart drunk."

Casey speaks up again. "Who says that?"

"*They* said it," the guy says. "Just *they.*"

The group cracks up.

"I want to see that study," Casey says. "It's a crock. Brittany is not stupid, and Rick is not all that smart. That's my point. You're not yourselves when you're sloppy drunk. But it's okay. I'll drive you all home and make sure you don't get into trouble."

"Can't be fun for you."

Casey just laughs.

"I don't think Casey would be a sloppy drunk," Brittany says. "I think she'd be a neat drunk, and what fun is that?"

I can't imagine why Brittany would have posted this video on her own page. I guess she thinks it's funny that her speech is slurred and her thinking is hindered. She probably thinks the conversation is somehow profound.

I go back to Casey's page. She didn't post anything that day. She didn't even tag that video so it would show up on her page, even though it makes her look good.

I try to imagine that girl on the screen who's nonjudgmental about her friends and amused at their stupidity, brutally murdering one of them. It doesn't compute.

I almost like the girl I've seen. She's cute and seems sweet, and I don't sense any cynicism or undertone of anger. I wonder if her aversion to losing control is because of past consequences when drunk. Maybe she knows it changes her personality. Makes her snap. But there's no evidence anywhere of that.

PTSD still reigns heavy in my mind as a possible contributor. She could have encountered some trigger that made her react and kill Brent accidentally. But his murder seemed so vicious, so planned. His injuries were in lethal places . . . his carotid artery, his spleen . . . as if she knew exactly where to cut him to bleed him out faster.

But she wouldn't have taken off if she had nothing to hide. She *must* be the killer.

19

DYLAN

Since I have no leads on where Casey might be, and the Pace family insists I keep looking for her, I go talk to her older sister, Hannah. As I drive up, she's out in her small front yard playing with her baby, who's sitting in a tiny plastic pool full of floating toys, splashing water. Hannah's clothes are wet, but she sits on the concrete beside the pool. She looks at me suspiciously as I pull into her driveway and get out of the car. Her hand goes out to steady her child.

"Hi," I say. "My name's Dylan Roberts. I'm working for the Pace family. I was wondering if I could ask you a few questions."

Hannah doesn't move from her crouch. "You have any ID?" she asks.

I show her my credentials. She glances at my name, then says, "I've told the police everything I know. I don't know where my sister is."

"Can we still talk?" I ask. "I'm just trying to get a clear picture of what happened with Brent Pace." I squat down next to the pool. "See, Brent was a good friend of mine. We grew up together. I'm just trying to make some sense out of it."

Hannah pulls the baby out of the pool, throws a towel around her. "I'm sorry about your friend," she says grudgingly as she dries her. "I met Brent several times. He was a nice guy. A really good friend to Casey." She gets up with her baby. "I have to go. Have to get her dressed."

I smile at the baby, who's kicking to get down and grinning at me like she knows me. "How old is she?" I ask.

Hannah looks at me as though she doesn't know whether to answer. "She's six months old. Why?"

"Just curious," I say. "It's been a long time since I've been around a baby. It's hard to judge age." I hold out my hand and the little girl grabs my finger. "She's really cute," I say. "Looks just like you."

Hannah softens the slightest bit. "Look, I really don't have anything to talk to you about."

"Please. I wanted to ask you some things about your father."

"My father." I half expect her to turn and run, but that perks her up, and finally she says, "Okay, come in."

Inside, she throws a T-shirt over the little girl's bathing suit and settles her on the floor with her toys. "I'm only letting you in because I want you to understand," she says. "I don't talk about my father. His suicide was upsetting and I don't like dredging it up."

"Your mother thinks it was homicide."

Hannah stares at me. "My mother has issues."

I've investigated suicides several times in my career in the military. In every single case, their close friends and family members didn't want to believe it unless there was a note or something they couldn't deny. Hannah's break from that pattern throws me. "I'm really sorry for his death," I say. "I'm sure it was hard on the family."

"It was hardest on Casey," Hannah says.

I've heard that before, so I'm not surprised. "I just want to know, did it change her?"

That turns Hannah's face red. "Not in the way you want to hear me say. She didn't become a psychopathic killer, if that's what you mean."

"I'm not suggesting anything like that. I'm just wondering . . . did she have depression, anxiety, anything like that as a result?"

She shakes her head. "We were all depressed for a couple years after that. We were all anxious. Waiting for the other shoe to drop."

The other shoe? I tilt my head. "What do you mean by that?"

She's bending over her baby, but her head snaps up. "Nothing. I just mean that it was a bad time in our lives."

I'm quiet for a minute, processing.

"Listen, my sister didn't do what they're saying. Casey is the bravest, most decent person I know."

I watch her as she picks up her baby and heads to the adjoining kitchen. She gets a teething ring from the fridge and gives it to her.

"Have you heard from Casey?" I ask.

She won't look at me. "I told the police already that I don't know where she is."

"But have you *talked* to her?" I repeat.

"No!" Hannah says finally. "You're barking up the wrong tree. If Brent were here he would tell you. She would never hurt anyone, much less a good friend."

"Did your sister have any drug problems? Alcohol?"

"Not at all," she says. "She doesn't drink or use drugs. She's never liked losing control."

That's pretty much what I'd gleaned from the video. I step toward the kitchen counter. "I asked your mother this. Do you have a theory about who killed Brent?"

Hannah lets out a bitter laugh, but then she seems to catch herself. "I've said all I'm gonna say. I have nothing else to add. I have to ask you to leave."

As I'm walking out, I see an empty box on the floor by the wall. I glance at the FedEx label—it came from Seattle. Was it from Casey? What could have been in it? "If I could just ask you a few more questions—"

"Sorry," she says, coming around the counter and opening the door for me. "I need you to go."

I don't like overstaying my welcome, even when I'm doing a job. I can be tough when I have to, but this is not the time, so I let her show me out. I linger in the doorway and look back at the box long enough to read the address label: Hannah Boon, c/o Sam and Cheryl Boon. The company that shipped it is Jack's Sporting Goods in Seattle, handwritten. I try to see the address when Hannah blocks my view. I bend down to pick it up, but Hannah sees what I'm doing and jerks it away.

As she closes the door behind me, I stand on her porch for a moment, staring down at the little pool. Sam and Cheryl Boon. FedEx. If I were Casey and needed to get something to my sister, I might send it to a relative. Someone who would get the box to her without being suspicious.

I go to my car and open my laptop, link to my phone's personal hotspot, then check out the Boons. They're Hannah's husband's parents. Intent on getting the information from FedEx about where the package originated, I start my car and pull away.

Is Casey still around here somewhere, maybe even at the Boons', hiding in plain sight? Or did she just use them as a delivery address?

20

DYLAN

The girl at FedEx has a flirty smile, and when I tell her that I'm working with the police on a case, she seems even more interested in me. I play along, grinning back and leaning toward her on the counter like I'm about to ask for her number.

"Do y'all know who killed that guy?" she asks, eyes big. "They're saying it was a girl."

I give her a coy look. "You know I'd love to tell you, but then I'd have to kill you."

She laughs like she's never heard that before, and I sort of hate myself for using such an overdone joke. "Seriously, I need to trace a package. Can you help me with that?"

"Depends," she says.

I know this game. It's the one where she dangles the information carrot, and I offer to take her for coffee. She can't tell by looking at me that I'm a nightmare in relationships, that I start out strong, then drift so far into myself that no one can reach me.

My shrink tells me I have insight into my mental state, that it's a good indicator of an eventual recovery. Tell that to the women I've hurt. Though I long for an end to the loneliness, I don't want to take anyone else down on the way.

She seems like a nice girl; I change my body language so I won't lead her on. I get to the point and ask her to do a search for packages sent to Hannah Boon in the last month.

She pretty quickly comes up with the package sent to her via her in-laws. It was the box I saw from Seattle. I've already checked to see if there really is a Seattle company called Jack's Sporting Goods. I found nothing. "Where did the package originate from?" I ask. "I mean, not what was on the Sender line, but the FedEx office it was shipped from."

She does a little looking, then sucks in a breath. "Oh my gosh. It's not from Seattle. This was sent from one of our Atlanta stores." She looks at me like she's just saved the day. "Do you think that's where that killer is?"

I give her a look that reminds her I can't say, but I know she interprets it as more flirting. "Can you do a search of any packages sent from Hannah Boon in the last month?"

Eager to help more, she clicks away. Finally, she turns her screen where I can see it. "Yes, she sent a package just a few days ago to someone named Liz Harris in New York. Do you think the killer's in New York?"

I ignore the question this time. "Can you look up that recipient and see her history? Has she shipped or received packages before?"

She looks excited, as if I've just thought of a genius plan.

"Yes! Liz Harris has been getting packages at that address for three years. Before that, she had a Shreveport address. Is this the killer?"

"No," I say firmly, hoping she doesn't consider this grist for the gossip mill. I think for a moment.

So Hannah's package—the cardboard box I saw—could have come from Casey. Why else would it have a fake Sender address? But that doesn't mean Hannah's shipment went to Casey. If Liz is a real person with a history at that address, the package probably had nothing to do with Casey.

Still . . . the timing of Hannah's package going to Liz Harris could be important—just a couple of days after she received the Jack's Sporting Goods box. "Do me a favor," I say, glancing at her name tag. "Linda, could you give me printouts of the packages sent immediately before and after the one Hannah Boon sent to New York?"

She gets right on it. "You're really good," she says as she types. "I would never think of all this."

"That's why they pay me the big bucks," I tease.

"Here they are." She prints them out and hands them to me. "Anything?"

They're both from different people.

"Were either of these paid for with the same credit card Hannah used on the Liz Harris package?"

She checks. "No. Both were paid for with cash."

I study the addresses. The package sent before the one to New York was a return to Pottery Barn. The one sent immediately after was to Grace Newland at an Atlanta hotel.

Pay dirt. The sender is listed as John Smith. Hannah isn't very creative.

Grace Newland. Could that be the name Casey is going by?

"Linda, you've been amazing. Just what I needed."

She beams. "Anytime. Seriously. If you need anything else, just call." She jots down her cell number and I take it.

"Listen, don't talk about this, okay? We don't want anyone tipped off."

"I never would," Linda says, but I doubt she can contain it.

"I mean it," I tell her. "You could be charged with obstruction of justice."

Her smile fades. "Oh. Wow. I won't say a thing."

When I leave FedEx, I head to the police department and go up to the Major Crimes Unit, where Gordon Keegan sits at his desk talking on the phone. I lift my hand in a wave, and he takes his feet off his desk and motions for me to come over. I take a seat on a folding chair in his cubicle and wait for him to get off.

Finally, he hangs up and shakes my hand. "Please tell me you've found her."

"I might have," I say. "I have an address in Atlanta where she may have received a package."

For some reason I can't quite name, I decide not to tell him about the name Grace Newland. It may be a false lead, but that's not really why I hesitate to share it. Maybe it's a pride thing. I want to find her before he does.

"I need to go there and see if she's at that hotel. I checked the schedule and the next flight to Atlanta is in two hours. Can you let the Atlanta police know I'll be coming? I may need them to help me make an arrest."

"Absolutely," he says.

"One other thing. I still need the file on her father's death."

"Whose father's death?"

"Casey's. The suicide?"

He stares at me blankly for a moment. "Oh, right."

"I'd especially like to see any video of Casey's interview after finding her dad. That could tell me something about her mind, her emotions. Like why she might have snapped and murdered a friend."

He scratches his eyebrow with the back of his thumb. "Okay. Yeah. Might take some time. I'm kind of up to my eyeballs."

Not satisfied, I try again. "It's just that I talked to her mother, who insists Andy Cox didn't kill himself. That it was murder."

151

"The mother's a mental case," he says. "Probably why he offed himself."

His callous sentiment strikes me.

"Look, just go to Atlanta," he says. "If you find her, the file won't matter. If you don't, I'll shoot it to you."

I was hoping to study the file on the plane, but I can see that he isn't budging on that, so I head to the airport.

The flight is only an hour and a half, and when I arrive and turn my phone back on, I see that I have a text from Keegan, telling me the name of my contact at the Atlanta PD in case someone needs to verify my credentials. I rent a car and head to the hotel where the package was received.

After explaining who I am, I show Casey's picture to the woman at the front desk, and she narrows her eyes. "Yeah, I think I've seen her. I recognize those eyes."

"She may be going by the name Grace Newland. Is she still here?"

She types something into the computer, then shakes her head. "No, she checked out the day before yesterday."

"What else does it show? Did she have a vehicle? A tag number? Did she receive any other packages?"

She looks at her file, then shrugs. "She wrote that she was driving a white Kia. I didn't get a model or tag. That's all we ask for. And she received one package, which she picked up right before she checked out."

"Credit card?"

"She paid cash," she says.

Disappointed, I look around at the ceiling corners. "Do you have cameras in the hallways? In the parking lot?"

"Yes," she says.

"I'll need to see the video of those days." Maybe I can see her tag number, or any changes she's made to her appearance.

The girl checks in the back, and I hear her talking on the phone. Finally, she comes back. "I'm sorry, but it's on a two-day cycle. After a couple of days it's recorded over. We don't have that day."

I can't believe it. "Why have a security camera if you do that?"

"Because most of the crimes in the hotel are reported within twenty-four hours. We keep the video long enough for that. I'm really sorry."

Unbelievable. I ask her if Casey asked for directions or a map, or said anything about where she was going. She says she doesn't remember talking to her.

I find the business center. Maybe she left a trail on the computer. Nothing significant comes up in its history. Maybe she didn't use it. By now she probably bought a computer of her own. She seems to have cash. I wonder where she got it. Is someone helping her?

I can't believe I've come to another dead end. How can this keep happening?

She could have gone anywhere—north or south, farther east, back west. She doesn't have family or friends in Georgia that I've been able to trace. But that might be precisely why she ended up here.

Before going back to the airport, I check with the bus and train stations. Another dead end.

Casey Cox is smarter than the average fugitive. She might be smarter than me.

21

CASEY

There's a woman who sits out in the courtyard of Gran's Porch, rocking in a chair that squeaks with every forward thrust. She seems lost, as if she woke up this morning and found herself in a strange place and can't find her way home.

I can't stand to see people lonely, so I walk outside my little cottage room and approach her.

"Hi," I say, slipping my hair behind my ears, something I always do when I'm nervous. "I'm Grace. Mind if I sit down?"

She seems to snap out of her deep reverie. "It's not mine. It's here for everybody, but nobody ever uses it this time of year. Too humid, they say. Like they expect Georgia to be Ottawa."

I take that as a yes, so I sink into a pollen-covered Adirondack chair. I don't lean back. "I like it here. It's good for the skin, right?"

She smiles as she looks at me now. "Southern girl, huh? I took you to be a Yankee."

I haven't heard anyone use that word since some book I read in fifth grade.

"Where are you from?" she asks.

I try to remember Grace Newland's history. "Oklahoma," I say weakly.

She looks at me like I just appeared from the moon. "No way. You sound like me. Deep South, not cowboy."

She's got a deeper accent than mine, I hope, but I don't correct her. "I've lived a few other places along the way. In the South."

"Can't be a very long way. You're too young."

How did we get here so fast? Maybe I made a mistake coming out here. I stand back up, straighten my jeans. "Anyway . . . I just thought I'd say hi."

"You don't have to run off," she says quickly. "For heaven's sake, sit down."

I hesitate for a minute, then slowly lower back down.

"My name's Sealy," she says.

"Hi, Sealy." I try to redirect the conversation. "Are you traveling through?"

"Traveling? Me? No, I live here."

"All the time?" I ask.

"That's right," she says briskly. "You got a problem with that?"

"No. It's a nice place to live."

She broods for a moment as she stares toward the parking lot. "It used to be nice. Folks who opened it were this decent family, did everything themselves. Treated the guests like they were royalty. Real homey-like. Then they died, and their ungrateful kids sold it off to some corporation somewhere. Owners have prob'ly never seen the place. Cigar face in there runs it now and couldn't care less."

I want to ask her why she lives here then, why she doesn't just go get an apartment or a house if she has enough to pay a weekly motel rate. But I don't want to rile her again. "There's bird poop on that chair," I mutter, pointing to the chair across from me.

"Been there forever. Nobody ever cleans this area."

I get up. "I'll be right back." I go into my room and get a washcloth, wet it and scrub soap on it, then grab a bottled water. I take them back to the courtyard. Sealy looks up at me.

"I can take care of this right now," I say. I kneel in front of the chair and scrub off the caked bird droppings. "What kind of birds do you see here?"

"I don't know," she says. "I don't notice birds."

"Really?" I ask as I scrub. "I love birds. We had these two cardinals that used to hang around my backyard when I was a kid. I loved when they came. It was like a bright-colored message. Oh, and my mom always has these hummingbird feeders out. Lots of them, really. She kind of collects them. She collects everything, actually. But these hummingbirds just float there, their wings moving so fast they're invisible. I love watching them. They should get a hummingbird feeder here."

"Then there'd be more of *that* on the seats."

"Comes off easy," I say, moving so she can see my work. The chair is now suitable for sitting in. "You could hang it off to the side, over the grass. It's fun to watch them."

"Management would never buy the food. Probably wouldn't even let me hang one."

I have another friend like Sealy, back home in Shreveport. You would think that Molly would be the name of someone light and fluffy. But Molly sees only the dark side of the world, the part that shows on negative film. She misses all the good stuff.

I get her perspective. But I respond to life differently. I feel challenged to see beyond that dark part and find the good stuff. I take pleasure in pointing out the bright sides to Molly, because when I do, I remind myself they exist. Maybe Sealy can be my new Molly.

Later, when I go out, I stop by a hardware store and buy a hummingbird feeder. Not thirty, like my mom has. Just one will do. I mix up the sugar water when I get back, fill it to the line, then take it outside. I hang it from a lower branch on an unhealthy tree in the courtyard.

It's a shock of red in a colorless place. I wish I could paint the chairs some bright color. That might make Sealy smile.

She's inside now, and I grin at the thought that she'll see the feeder the next time she comes out to sit. I hope the hummingbirds give her a show. The thought lifts the heaviness that weighs on me like an oversized wool cloak.

I sleep better tonight than I have since this whole thing began.

22

DYLAN

There's one thing you need to know. Brent Pace loved Casey Cox."

The declaration comes from Brent's best friend Kip, a co-worker and fellow reporter at the *Shreveport Times*, who hung out a lot with Brent when they weren't working. I know this from asking around and from studying Brent's Facebook page.

"Loved her?" I ask. "Did they ever date?"

"No," Kip says. "Casey didn't feel the same. I mean, she always told him she loved him, but she told all of us that. She made it clear that she thought of him as a friend."

"Brent was okay with that?"

"I think he felt like Casey was wounded. That if he helped her heal, she could finally move on and see him as more."

I know what he means by "wounded," but I want to hear his take on it. "Wounded in what way?"

"Her dad's death," he says. "It haunted her. Don't get me wrong. She wasn't morose. She didn't mope around about it. She's always friendly and upbeat, and she doesn't talk about it. But he told me she let her guard down with him once and opened up about it. He couldn't stop thinking about it."

"I have a theory about Casey," I say. "I'm thinking she might have PTSD. It would stand to reason after finding her dad the way she did. Did she ever have extreme reactions to things? Did she talk of nightmares? Were there things she did that didn't make sense?"

He considers that. "I know she didn't sleep much. A friend, Molly, lived with her for a few weeks and said she would hear her talking in her sleep, crying out after a dream. She didn't date much. She seemed to keep men at a distance, like she had some hang-up about being that vulnerable. Lots of guys were interested, but they never got anywhere. Brent just hung in there. All of his work in the last few weeks was about her."

"His work? What do you mean?"

"He was going back through the investigation of her dad's death."

I plant my elbows on the table, lean forward. "So how was he doing that?"

"He kind of dug into the story like it was an article he was working on. Brent always was great with research. He used his off-hours to dig."

"What exactly was he digging for?"

"I don't know, just answers to what really happened. He said Casey thought her dad was murdered, and he was trying to prove it. He was interviewing people, trying to find out what happened in the days before her dad's death, I guess to give her some kind of closure. One time he told me that Casey already suspected who the killer was, but that there was nothing she could do about it."

"He told you that? Did he say who?"

"No, he acted like he realized he had just let something slip. He didn't go any further."

I make a note of that. "Did he ever send any information to you, any copies of things he had recorded?"

"No," he says. "We didn't get that detailed. Like I said, he worked on it off the clock."

Didn't Keegan tell me the police had logged Brent's laptop and desktop computers, as well as his phone? Maybe they haven't had time to look through the files yet. I make a note to ask them if I can take a look.

"The thing is, Casey's too smart to do any of this," Kip says. "I mean, even if by some bizarre chance she did want to kill somebody, she was smarter than to do it like this. She wouldn't have left her footprints all over the crime scene. She wouldn't have made it look like she was so guilty. She's way too smart for that, and that's why you haven't found her yet."

He makes a good point. "You got a theory?"

He shrugs. "I didn't see the crime scene. I don't know what evidence the police have, other than what we've reported. All I know is what I know of Casey, and she is not a killer."

I sip my coffee for a moment, looking down at the table. "You know, sometimes people have mental issues you can't see. Sometimes they snap and do things they wouldn't ordinarily do. If somebody is upset or traumatized, sometimes an event triggers something . . . takes them back to another time when life was out of control, and they act out in unpredictable ways. That's how PTSD works."

Kip rubs his chin. "I guess. But if you knew Casey . . ."

Everyone keeps saying that, so I make up my mind to get to know her better. Back home, I look for more photos and videos, this time on her sister's Facebook page. I can't imagine why she hasn't made her page private after all the media attention, but I'm able to see everything posted there. There's a video taken at Hannah's birthday party. Casey has her baby niece on her lap and is making her giggle as Hannah videotapes. Casey is clearly enraptured with the child. Her eyes are bubbly, happy, though now and again when the camera catches her I see shadows behind her gaze.

I search for Casey videos on the social media of every friend of Casey's I can find, cross-referencing all of their friends. I strike out on several that don't have Casey in them, but then I find one that tags her, and I quickly click on it. Up comes a party, and I find Casey sitting on the edge of a picnic table, being interviewed about a friend's wedding.

"When Barbie met you, Jake," she says to the camera, "I worried that you weren't good enough for her, but then I got to know you, and I saw how you protect her and how sweet you are and how you put her needs first, and before long, I thought, 'This is the perfect relationship.' You two are so compatible. They say opposites attract, but I think *similars* attract."

"Similars," Brent says, stepping up behind her. "That's not a word."

"It's a word now," Casey says. "I just used it. Didn't you hear me?"

Brent laughs, and Casey goes on. "Seriously, you guys are so much alike, I bet you'd test exactly the same on all those compatibility tests. You're perfect for each other, and I mean that in a good way. I know if I look you up in thirty years, you're still going to be together. I look forward to all those anniversary parties." Her voice cuts off as she dabs at tears in her eyes.

Brent nudges Casey. "You act like you're never gonna see them again. Like the minute they say 'I do' they'll go poof and vanish. After the wedding, we're all still gonna hang out, you know."

Casey smiles. "Maybe. Things change, but that's okay. They need to focus on each other. Now they're building a family." She looks back into the camera. "Guys, it's gonna be awesome. I hope someday I can find somebody like Jake."

In the background, Brent points to himself and shrugs, as though telling the camera, and anyone who would watch it later, that he's available. I'm sure Casey saw it later. I wonder if she realized before then that he was a contender.

That was Brent, I think. He would hang out with a girl for months before making his move, almost like he was certain he'd lose her as a friend if he tagged her as a girlfriend.

I let the video play through several other interviews and I see that this is something that probably played at the engaged couple's reception, the rehearsal dinner, something the couple could take home and cherish forever. But Casey's declaration is the best of all. It's heartfelt and sweet and doesn't hold a morsel of malice or sarcasm.

I skim through other videos, see her being adventurous, swinging from a vine and dropping into a ravine full of water, screaming all the way. Many of them show the younger Casey, when she was in her teens. She wasn't afraid of risk.

She's in the background of several of her friends' videos at other events and outings. She always seems happy and smiling, engaging, talking less than others, listening most.

Before I know it, three hours have passed, and I realize that I like what I've learned of Casey today. I agree it isn't normal for her to have snapped and killed somebody. She doesn't seem like a ticking bomb.

In fact, I wish I had a friend like her, or at least the way she appears to be. I could use that right now. I hate the thought of putting someone like her in prison, but if she killed my child-hood friend, then that's where she needs to be.

It keeps coming back to her father's death. There have to

be clues hiding there. Since Brent was working on that when he died, maybe following the same trail he followed will lead me to her.

⌒

Monday morning I show up at the police department unannounced and go to the third floor where Keegan sits in his cubicle. He's wearing headphones, watching his laptop screen. It's a homemade video of a woman being interviewed. He doesn't notice me as I walk toward him. "Detective," I say.

He swings around, jerking the headphone cord out of the laptop. The audio switches to the computer's speakers, and I hear Brent's voice asking the woman a question. I don't hear his whole question, but I hear the name *Andy Cox*. Keegan quickly closes his laptop. "Dylan, my man! I didn't know you were coming by today," he says, overbright, springing up and extending a hand as though he's happy to see me. "Tell me you've found our girl."

"Not yet," I say. "But maybe you can help with that."

He sits back down. "Shoot."

"I was talking to one of Brent's friends from work and I found out that Brent was working on a case."

"What do you mean, a case? He wasn't a cop."

"But he was a journalist. He was trying to uncover some of the mystery involving Casey Cox's father's death."

Suddenly Keegan sits straighter, and I can see I've hit a

nerve. "You're overstepping again, Dylan," he says in a low voice, glancing around as if making sure no one heard. This guy's ego is massive. "You have been hired for a specific purpose, and that's to find Casey Cox."

"But I don't know where she is right now," I say, keeping my voice as low as his. "The Paces insist that I stay on the case, so I'm doing what I can to get inside her head."

The tips of his ears redden, then a pink color fades across his shaved head. His chin is rigid as he leans toward me, biting out words. "Why. Are. You. Talking. To. Brent's. Friends?"

I'm not intimidated, despite his best effort. What is it with this guy? "Because they were her friends too, Detective. I'm not a bird dog sent to retrieve the prey. You haven't found her, so I'm trying to."

Keegan fixes me with a long, piercing stare that has accusations behind it. I'm just not sure what I'm being accused of.

"Anyway," I say, unflapped, "what is the problem with my seeing Andy Cox's file?"

"The problem is that I don't need some rookie PI digging up video of Casey Cox looking all sympathetic and pitiful. I don't want a jury deciding that it's no wonder this kid turned into a simmering pot that blew thirteen years later."

"You don't think a good defense attorney would dig that up anyway?"

"Look, Dylan, I'm knee-deep in evidence that has to be turned over to the DA so he can prosecute when we find her. I don't have time to dig up a thirteen-year-old suicide case. Of course his crazy widow doesn't want to believe he checked out on her. Families always go into denial."

"True, but since Brent was working on that, don't you think it's relevant?"

Keegan stares at me for a longer moment, then shakes his head. "I've given you an answer, Dylan. You're not on the force. You have no reason to be prying into an old case that was closed years ago. Now, I suggest that if you can't find Casey, you let the Paces know that you've come to a dead end, because they're wasting their money on you."

That strikes me as odd. Doesn't *he* want her found? "I'll find her," I say. "And you don't have to dig it up for me. I can go to Chief Gates. He's friends with the Paces, and he wants her found. He can get the Cox file and the files from Brent's computers pulled."

Keegan has begun to sweat, beads over his lip. "Don't bother him. He's strung too tight. I don't want him on my case." He pulls out a handkerchief and wipes his forehead. "All right, let me see what I can do," he says finally. "Maybe I can give you some of it even if I don't give you all of it. But I'm telling you now it won't help you. She was twelve years old. It was a long time ago. If you're trying to excuse what she did with Brent—"

"Not at all," I cut in. "I'm just trying to explain it. Why a girl who, by all accounts, was a loyal friend suddenly snaps and brutally murders someone. If I'm going to find her, I just need to understand."

"But she did it," Keegan says. "There's evidence all over the place. I logged it myself. We don't need to hand the Defense their case."

"But why did she do it? " I ask. "That's what I need to know."

"No, that's not really what you need to know," he says. "What you need to know is where she is. I would've found her by now if I had the time and money. You're supposed to be a pro. Do your job. Bring her back here so we can lock her up once and for all."

His dismissive attitude irks me. Then I mentally shake myself. He's just an overworked cop trying to get justice for my dead friend.

I take the stairs down to the first floor, and as I head for the exit I notice an old woman going into the evidence room. She looks familiar, and it hits me that she's the woman who was being interviewed in the video Keegan was watching. I pause at the door, wondering if I should go in and talk to her, but then I hear footsteps on the stairs above me. I glance up and see Keegan coming down.

I realize he'd never tolerate my going into the evidence room without his blessing. I'll just come back later.

23

CASEY

If you have to take the first job that comes along in a town you've never been to, you could do a lot worse than a counter job at Simmons Cell Repair. I like the people I work with, though they find each other difficult.

One of the college students my boss mentioned in my interview is really a sixty-nine-year-old widow named Cleta who's trying to get a business degree. She loves changing the radio station in the store to fifties music, to which she dances and shakes her hips as she moves around the store.

The other one, Rachel, really is of college age—twenty or

so—and she marches to a different drum. She sits at the counter today, deeply engrossed in drawing on the inside of her forearm with a gel pen. "What are you doing?" I ask.

"Giving myself a tattoo," she mutters, distracted.

"You already have one."

"It's not real," Cleta says from the other side of the store. "At least not all of it."

I'm not sure I understand. I step over to Rachel and study the paisley design on her left arm. "Just some of it's real?"

"Yeah," Rachel says, carefully tracing over the faded ink. "I went for a real tattoo, but it hurt. I hate pain. Wound up with part of the design before I got sick and had to quit."

"So do you draw the rest in every day?"

"Yeah. If I don't, it just looks like I've been writing on myself."

"You *have* been writing on yourself."

"Yeah, but when I do this, it's art."

I smile, glad I've never gotten a tat. "I have a friend who got a Chinese saying tattooed on her calf. She didn't even know what it said."

Rachel looks up. "Did she find out?"

"Yeah, a while later. It said, 'Exit to the right.'"

"What? Why would she have that?"

"Probably someone's joke," I say. "But what if it had said something profound, but something she profoundly disagreed with? Like, what if she quoted the Qur'an, then became a Christian? Or what if she quoted the Beatles, then decided she hated their music? My dad was like that. He'd loved the Grateful Dead since he was a teenager, but then when he started playing their stuff for me, he didn't like them anymore. What if he'd had Deadhead etched on his skin, only to find that he wasn't one at all?"

Rachel looks up at me, amused. "You think too much," she says.

"Yeah, I've been told that before."

We laugh a lot together, and it feels good to have new friends. The work isn't hard. The learning curve has been easy, since I read the manuals of all the phones and practiced how to work them in the store my first day. I've picked up enough to wait on customers and check in their phones.

"Do you think the person who dropped this phone in the toilet cleaned it off before he brought it to us?" Cleta asks, putting a damaged device into a Ziploc bag.

"Doubtful," Rachel says. "It's not like swabbing it with alcohol would be the first thing on their mind."

"Gross," I say. "Do we have alcohol wipes?"

"No, but we should so get some," Rachel says, looking up from her tattoo. "Do you know how many different kinds of bacteria are on people's cell phones? E. coli, staph, botulism . . ."

"I thought botulism was food poisoning," I say.

"Still . . . you name it, it's on those phones. Once I got a boil on my finger that swelled up like a basketball. I swear it was because of the germs on somebody's phone."

I grin. "Like a basketball? Really?"

"Well, maybe like a melon."

"It was a golf ball," Cleta corrects. "More like a ping-pong ball."

"That's still pretty big," I say.

"We should wear gloves," Rachel adds. "Seriously, it should be a requirement of this job."

"We could if we wanted, right?"

"Yeah, but I never do things I don't have to do."

I can't help laughing. They both crack me up.

24

DYLAN

I go back to the police department after lunch, and when I've made sure Keegan isn't on the first floor, I quickly push into the evidence room. The place is dimly lit and smells of dust and mold. The little woman I saw earlier—the one from the video Keegan was watching—is sitting at the desk, trying to open a bottle of pills. I wait quietly and watch as she gets the bottle open, pours some out in her shaking hand, and throws them into her mouth. She gulps down a glass of water, then puts the bottle of pills into her purse.

She shoves her reading glasses higher on her nose, chains hanging from each side.

Though I'm only a few feet away, she hasn't heard me come in. I walk quietly across the floor and stand in front of her like a student waiting for his teacher to acknowledge him. The plaque on her desk says Sara Meadows.

Finally, she pulls her glasses down her nose and looks up.

"Hi," I say. "I'm Dylan Roberts. I'm a private investigator working with the department on the Brent Pace case."

Her eyes narrow, and she takes her glasses off now, lets them drop to her chest. "Do Detectives Keegan and Rollins know that?" she asks in a smoker's voice.

"Yes, ma'am, they know. I've been hired by the Pace family to find the girl they believe killed their son. I understand you knew Brent."

She sits up straighter and looks at the door, as if expecting someone else to come through. Her eyes are dull as she moves her gaze back to me. "How do you understand that?"

"I knew Brent. We were friends since childhood. That's why his family hired me." I know that doesn't answer her question, but I'm hoping it will make her trust me.

She's already pale, but I watch her blanch even more. "I . . . I don't know who you're talking about. Are you *allowed* in here?"

"I have some police privileges," I say.

She tries to get up, knocks her chair over. It crashes to the floor, and I lunge to catch her before she falls. A metal door opens at the back of the room behind her desk, and another small woman rushes to the front. "Sara? Are you okay, hon?"

Ms. Meadows rights herself and reaches for the chair, but she can't quite bend to get it. I set it up for her.

"Excuse me," she says in that shredded voice. "I need a minute."

"Sure, hon," her coworker says. "You go back and lay down. I'll take over here."

Ms. Meadows hobbles to the back.

"May I help you?" the other woman asks.

"Is she all right?" I ask in a low voice. "I just wanted to talk to her, but she doesn't seem well."

The woman leans across the desk. "Cancer," she whispers. "She's worked here so long. She insists on still coming in, but she's in stage four."

That explains the meds.

"I'll help you," she offers. "What do you need?"

I draw in a deep breath. "I really just wanted to talk to Ms. Meadows. I'll come by later."

"Yes, do. She'll probably be okay after she rests a little." She drops her voice to a whisper. "We have a cot back there for her. Honestly, I don't know why she doesn't want to be at home. If it were me . . ."

"I'm surprised the department allows her to stay," I say quietly.

"Chief Gates refuses to let her go," she says. "He says she has a place here as long as she wants it. Bless her heart. Do you want me to give her a message?"

I'm not sure I want to give her my name. Keegan might

hear that I was here. "No, that's okay. I'll talk to her later. Let her rest."

I leave the department and get lunch. An hour or so later, I go back to the department, again careful to avoid Keegan as I slip into the evidence room.

Ms. Meadows is back at her desk. She looks up when I come in, and this time she glances toward the back as if making sure we're alone. When I reach her desk, she says, "What do you want?"

I keep my voice low. "I know that you did an interview with Brent Pace before his death. I wanted to talk to you about it."

She swallows nervously, then gets up and turns away. She picks up the file she's working on and slips it into a tall cabinet behind her. She stops to write on a Post-it note. When she comes back to the desk, she hands it to me.

"Be there at seven thirty tonight. I'll talk to you then."

My heart stumbles as I take the card and see her address. She turns away again, dismissing me. I want to tell her I'm sorry about her cancer, that I appreciate her agreeing to talk to me, but I can tell she wants me out of here. I slip out into the hall and hurry to my car.

At seven fifteen, I drive to Sara Meadows' house—a small Craftsman with an open carport. Her car is in the driveway. It's still light out, and her neighbor is working in the yard next door. I start to pull into the driveway, then I think better of it and park at the curb. I go to the cobwebby front door, ring the bell, then after a moment, knock hard in case she's hard of hearing.

A dog barks behind the door. Some of his barks flip to yelps, then lower to barking again. She doesn't come to the door, so I knock harder, ring the bell twice more. The dog is going crazy inside.

I walk around to the carport, find a side door, and knock on the glass. The dog changes rooms. He's closer and more frantic. There's no way the woman doesn't hear me.

"Can I help you?"

I swing around and see the next-door neighbor standing at the edge of the driveway, her pale blue capris dirty at the knees. "Oh, hi," I say. "I have an appointment with Ms. Meadows, but she's not answering her door. Have you seen her?"

She takes off her gloves. "I saw her come home from work. I know she's in there."

The dog keeps barking and yelping, as if in pain.

"Do you think she's all right? I know she's not well."

The neighbor knocks hard on the side door. "Sara?" she calls through the glass. "Sara, are you all right?"

I imagine it's the door to the kitchen. It's probably the door she uses most of the time.

"Sara?" The woman turns to me and says, "She's been getting sicker. She might not be able to get to the door. Let me call her." She pulls her cell phone out of her pocket and dials. We hear the phone ringing in the house, but no one answers.

Now I see the concern on her face. "Wait here," she says. "I'm going to get the key she gave me."

I wait as the woman disappears into her house, then comes

back. "Who did you say you are?" she asks as she puts the key in the lock.

"A friend from work," I say, not sure I want her to know my name.

The door opens and the woman steps inside. I wait on the steps as the dog goes nuts, yelping and barking and leaping in circles. Before she goes far, she bends over to stroke him, and he gets quiet.

The screen door closes behind her, and I can't see in as she walks farther into the house. I hope Ms. Meadows is just asleep after a long day of work in that dusty evidence room. If her neighbor wakes her up, she'll be groggy when we talk. Not ideal, but better than nothing.

Then I hear a scream.

I reach for the latch of the screen door as the neighbor comes stumbling out. She's already calling 911. "There's an emergency," she says into the phone. "My neighbor is bleeding on the floor. I think she's dead!"

Bleeding? From cancer?

I push past her into the house and find Sara Meadows lying in a pool of blood. I kneel and check her vitals. "Tell them there's no pulse," I yell to the neighbor.

I get on both knees and start to apply CPR, but then I see the bullet wound right over her heart. I look up and scan the room. There's a bullet hole through the back window.

Sara Meadows was murdered.

25

CASEY

"Grace, I think this phone is fine," Mr. Simmons tells me as he hands me an Android phone. "But click through it and make sure nothing needs to be restored. Check the calendar, the e-mail, the photos. If the last entries were weeks ago, or if the whole thing is empty, that tells you something. Also try to get online to see if the browser works."

People who drop their phones in water would be surprised to know that all they do here is wait for them to dry. Yes, the techs take the phones apart, remove the battery and all, but then they just wait it out. Often the phone comes on when they put it back together, and then they charge enough to make you think they did surgical magic on it.

He disappears into the back, and I lean on the counter and click around on the phone, hoping I don't botch this up. The calendar has recent entries, so that seems fine. When I check the owner's e-mail, new messages load, so that looks okay.

Finally, I click on Photos, and there's a long pause as it tries to load. I start to yell back to Mr. Simmons that this customer may have lost his photos, when a few pictures finally appear.

I click on one, and it fills the screen. It's a scruffy-looking man sitting at a kitchen table, drinking coffee. I start to advance to the next picture when my gaze snags on a newspaper on a buffet table behind him.

Even though it's tiny on the screen, I recognize the photo—it's Laura, Lucy's missing granddaughter. I zoom in and can just make out the headline. "Volunteers Search Forest for Missing Teen."

I frown. Miss Lucy told me they did those searches in the first weeks after Laura went missing, but none since. Why would this guy have kept that article for two years?

Maybe it's just an old picture. I check the date on the snapshot. It was taken last month.

My interest piqued now, I click through the rest of his pictures, studying details in his house. There's one photo of a towheaded baby in a bouncy seat. I click ahead to the next one—a fiftysomething woman who must be his wife, her blondish-gray hair piled on top of her head, bags under her eyes so puffy that she could carry cargo in them.

There, again, I see another article about Laura. This one says, "Shady Grove Teenager Missing."

Another two-year-old article lying around the house. Why?

I study the woman. She's wearing a tube top, definitely an odd choice for her age and size, but she's dressed it up with a pendant necklace.

It's one I've seen before—an old cameo pendant. I zoom in. It looks just like the one Laura Daly was wearing in the picture of her in her homecoming dress.

That's impossible. But then, cameos aren't exactly rare. Must be a coincidence. When I finish looking through his pictures, I open the owner's Internet browser and check his search history. Most people don't realize they've left open every article they've ever read. Sure enough, I see that his are all still there. Frowning, I flick through them. There are other articles about Laura, most of them over a year old. He must have read every article written about her on this phone.

Maybe he knows the family, or he's a relative or a neighbor. His fascination with Laura may be nothing more than concern over another Shady Grove citizen. But it bugs me.

I tell Mr. Simmons that the phone seems to be functioning correctly, but I dig for the customer's receipt and get his phone number and address. Frank Dotson. I'll ask Sandra if she knows him.

I make sure I'm out front when he comes to pick up the

phone. He still looks scruffy, unshaven for days, and his hair is scraggly and dirty. He smells like old cigarettes and body odor. His teeth are yellow, and one of the front ones is missing.

He seems way too interested in me, smiling and flashing that gap in his teeth, asking if I'm new in town. I tell him yes, that I just moved here.

"What brings you to Shady Grove?" he asks.

I hesitate for a moment, then decide to go for it. "I have friends here. The Dalys."

He blinks hard, then wipes the place above his lip where beads of sweat have burst out. "I don't believe I know them," he says.

I know that's not true. He's well acquainted with the Daly family, at least through articles about their missing daughter.

He leaves pretty quickly after that, and I shove his address into my pocket. Something isn't right about that guy or his wife. I may as well look into it. I don't have anything better to do.

26

DYLAN

think about leaving Sara Meadows' house before the police arrive, but since I went in and checked her vital signs, they'll want to know the details. Besides, I want to know what happened. Did someone kill her because she was going to talk to me?

The neighbor is hysterical and seems to have forgotten me. I stay in the carport, leaning against Ms. Meadows' car. When the first responders drive up, I meet them down the driveway, tell them who I am and that I'm working on a case with the department. I tell them what I know, then listen as they get the neighbor's account. They quickly declare it a crime scene and begin securing the area. Radio transmissions go crazy as everyone realizes it's Sara Meadows, the evidence lady they've all worked with.

"You say you had an appointment with her?" the first officer asks me.

I look toward the backyard, wondering if the killer had a hard time getting back there to take his shot. There is a gate, but it's open. "Yes. This afternoon we talked at the department. She asked me to come here at seven thirty." I pull out the Post-it note with her address, hand it to him. "I got here a little early, but no one came to the door. I didn't see anyone else. The neighbor was working in her yard. She is the one who called."

The neighbor is sobbing now, and I hear her telling the other officer that she didn't see anyone but me.

"What was it about?" my guy asks.

"What?"

"Your appointment? Why were you coming to talk to her?"

"As I said, I'm working with the department on the Brent Pace case. She knew Brent, so I wanted to talk to her about their last conversation."

I look toward the gate again. "Hey, I just noticed that back gate is open. Maybe the killer left footprints."

The cop looks toward it. "Listen, I need you to wait here. I'm sure the detectives are going to want to question you."

Right. I hope the detectives on rotation aren't Keegan and

Rollins, but even if not, those two will learn soon enough that I was talking to her. Keegan won't be happy.

But I don't take orders from him. I work for the Paces and at the pleasure of Chief Gates.

I hang around just outside the crime scene tape, sitting on the trunk of my car. I don't see any bullet holes or shattered glass in the front. I know the side door had been locked, because the neighbor checked it.

Up and down the street, neighbors have come out of their houses and stand in their yards talking quietly.

I try to work out what happened. One scenario comes to mind. Someone was waiting in the backyard for her to get home, and they could have had a silencer since her neighbor didn't hear it. Were they there when I was knocking on the door? How long before I arrived was she killed? Whoever it was clearly didn't want to rob her. They simply wanted her dead.

The more I think about it, the more I realize it couldn't have anything to do with me. No one except her coworker knew I had talked to her, and I doubt that it made a blip on her radar.

What had Sara Meadows been planning to tell me? More importantly, what was on the tape that Keegan was watching when I came into his office earlier?

After I give all my information to the detectives assigned to the case—who, thankfully, aren't Keegan and Rollins—they let me go, and I drive home and sit in my dark living room, staring at the wall.

I close my eyes as I remember other deaths, also bloody.

My buddies, laughing and trading barbs one second, blown into fragments the next.

I had tried to put them back together, tried to gather their parts . . . such a strange reaction. The shrinks repeatedly tell me they were gone, that nothing I could've done would've saved them. But I'm haunted by the thought that I did all the wrong things.

Some of that day is mercifully blank in my head, like how long it took for help to come. But I remember a shopkeeper just up the street, sweeping in front of his door and glancing toward us as though he'd just witnessed a fender bender. He just kept sweeping.

Death is attracted to me. It strikes at me often and misses, hitting those nearby.

I get hungry, but there's nothing in my fridge. I go out to get some fast food, but as I sit in the drive-through line waiting to place my order, I think about Hannah Boon, Casey's sister. If I tell her I found Sara Meadows dead after learning that she did an interview with Brent before his death—an interview about her father—will she talk more openly? I leave the line and drive over to Hannah's house. By now her husband's probably home, and she's probably trying to get the baby to bed. It's a terrible time, I know, but I have to talk to her.

A tall, lanky man answers the door with the baby on his hip. "Hey," he says, real friendly.

"Is Hannah here?" I ask, then realize that's rude. "I'm Dylan Roberts," I say. "I spoke to her Friday?"

His eyes suddenly go cold. "She's busy."

"It's really important," I say. "I was just about to interview someone who was involved in her father's case, and before I could talk to her, she was murdered."

He catches his breath, gapes at me, then disappears into the house. Hannah comes back with him. She approaches me reluctantly. "What?" she asks. "I've told you everything I know."

"Please, just a few more minutes," I say.

"Who died?" she demands to know.

"The clerk in the evidence room at the police department. Her name was Sara Meadows. She knew your father."

She mutters something to her husband. He takes the baby and disappears up the stairs. She steps outside and looks up and down the street, then steps back and lets me come in. I realize that anything I tell her could wind up being repeated back to Keegan, or maybe the department has had her house wired and can hear it right now. I have to be careful.

"I'm trying to follow Brent Pace's tracks for the days leading up to his murder," I say. "That trail led me to this woman who knew your father, and she had information about his death. She told me to meet her at her house tonight at seven thirty, but when I got there she was dead. Shot."

Tears rim Hannah's eyes, then she sets her chin, and her lips thin. She motions for me to follow her out to the backyard. There's a picnic table there, but she walks past it and takes me to a rustic, dirty bench at the back of the yard. "I'm not sure that I'm not being listened to," she says quietly.

She looks at me, desperate. "I have a child and husband. I can't risk having them come after me too. If they ask you, you've got to tell them that I wouldn't tell you a thing. That I'm convinced Dad killed himself."

"It's a deal," I say. "Just tell me what's going on."

"I don't know," she says, shaking her head. "Casey had all these theories, but I don't know if any of them were right. The only thing I can tell you is, you can't trust the people you're working with."

I frown. "I'm not working *with* anybody. I work by myself."

The back screen door scrapes open. Her husband steps out looking for us.

"I have to go," she says.

I take a chance as she walks away. "There was a videotape," I say. "I saw it on Keegan's computer screen. It was Brent interviewing Sara Meadows. I walked up on him, but when he saw me he shut it down. Didn't want me to see it."

She swings around. "If you find Casey, you're just gonna get her killed. They don't want her in prison. They want her dead, like everybody else who tries to expose them."

"I'm not looking just for Casey," I say. "I'm looking for the truth."

"But everything you think you know about the case is wrong. You've been lied to. The whole foundation of your investigation is a lie."

"I need to talk to her," I say.

She stares at me. "You said the woman is dead."

"I don't mean Sara Meadows. I mean Casey. Can you set up a meeting?"

"Of course not," she says. "I don't know where she is."

Her husband is still waiting. I step forward.

"I know that you mailed a package to her in Atlanta."

The color drains from her face.

"If you could give me just a phone number or an e-mail address. If I could talk to her briefly . . . It doesn't have to be in person."

"I told you no."

I can see that she won't budge, so I quickly jot down all my information—e-mail, cell phone, snail mail address, just in case she changes her mind. "Please. If she didn't do this murder, then maybe I can help."

Hannah laughs bitterly. "Yeah, we've heard that before." She points to the gate. "You can go out that way."

She marches toward her husband and back into the house, and I hear the deadbolt locking behind her.

27

CASEY

On my next day off, I take Highway 280 to Alabama. I pull off in Auburn and sit in a parking lot to call Hannah from my prepaid phone. If the police try to trace the signal, they'll see that it pings off an Auburn tower, and they'll assume I'm staying there. But I hope our precautions keep them from knowing about my calls. I'd rather die than get her into trouble.

I text her first. Can you talk?

In just a few minutes, she texts back. Not right now. In store with Emma. Call in one hour. You ok?

I write back, Yes. I'll call in an hour. Don't answer with your real phone nearby & don't be in your car.

Love you, she writes back.

I type, U2.

I use the hour to get fast food, then eat in my car, waiting for the time to pass. I'm not hungry. I force myself to chew and swallow, chew and swallow. I count the minutes. Is Hannah taking Emma to Mom? Will she have time to get to a safe place?

Finally, the hour is up. I call her back, and she answers quickly. "Is it okay now? Can you talk?" I ask her.

"Yes," she says in a voice just above a whisper. "I left Emma with Mom. I told her I had to run some errands. I'm walking at the park again. I just feel so paranoid, like I'm being watched."

"Trust me, you are. Where's your other cell phone?"

"In the car. Do you think they're bugging it?"

"They want to find me pretty bad. I don't want to get you into trouble."

"Casey, there are some things I need to tell you," she says, and I can hear her breath bumping as she walks. "The guy who's looking for you—the one the Pace family hired—is named Dylan Roberts. He came by the house again last night."

Dread burns like acid in my stomach. I wish I hadn't eaten. "What did he want?"

"He told me that he was trying to talk to a woman who was a file clerk or something in the police department. She knew Dad, and Brent had interviewed her before he died."

"Yes, I have the video," I say. "It was on the thumb drive you sent."

"He went to talk to her and found her shot dead."

That acid churns into nausea. Another death. When will this stop? Beads of sweat form over my lip.

"So he thought it was related to his talking to her?" I ask weakly.

"He didn't think anyone knew he was going."

"Is this guy Dylan working with Keegan?"

"He's working for the Paces," Hannah says, "and he realizes that some things aren't right. The woman's death freaked him out. He says he grew up with Brent—they were close friends—and he just wants to know the truth. He hinted that he understands that nothing may be the way it seems. Oh, and get this. He says that he walked up on Keegan and saw him watching the interview that Brent did with the woman."

I consider that for a moment. If Dylan told Hannah that, then he doesn't sound manipulative, just truly perplexed. "Do you think we can trust him?"

"Well, no. He's hired to find you."

"But I mean, could we trust him with the truth? Is he a decent person? Is he clean?"

Hannah blows out a long sigh. "I don't know. Honestly, he seems like the kind of person who wants to do the right thing, like he's really trying to get to the truth. But I'm not always the best judge of character."

"Maybe I should give the video to him," I say. "If I could send it anonymously from an e-mail address I create at the library or something . . ."

"If you want to, I've got his information. He gave me all his numbers and e-mail."

It won't hurt to take the info down, so I have her read it out to me.

"Casey, be careful. If you contact him, it might give them clues about where you are. Even now, just calling me . . ."

"It's okay," I tell her. "I drove out of state to make this call. It's pinging off towers that won't lead them to me. This phone isn't in my name. I've only used it for this. Next time I'll use a different one."

"You've thought all this out. How do you know to do all this?"

"I read a lot."

"This guy . . . he always seems respectful. I get the feeling that he's going to do the job he was hired for, but maybe you could trust him to get the truth out. You have to trust somebody if you ever hope to clear your name."

I don't tell her that I don't have a plan to clear my name. I just want to survive. As if she reads my thoughts, she says again, "Casey, you have to tell someone. You can't let them go on blaming you for this."

"If they can't find me, maybe that's enough to ask."

"No, that's not enough! We miss you." Her voice breaks, and I know she's crying. Hannah's usually a rock, and she never cries, so it really hurts to hear it. Her tone morphs into a higher pitch. "We want you to be able to come home. I can't stand the thought that we'll never see you again. Mom is so depressed.

She's buying things and cramming them into the house, constantly muttering and touching things. I'm trying to get her to the doctor, but there's such a long wait for an appointment. The longer this goes on, the worse she'll get, Casey."

"I know, but my getting killed or put in prison would be worse for her."

"It doesn't have to be one of those. There has to be a way to get the truth out. Maybe a reporter or something."

"Brent was a reporter." The reminder strikes her silent for a long moment.

I ask about Emma, and she sniffs through stories of her baby's latest milestones. I hang on as long as I can, not wanting to break the connection. It feels like my last grip on home, but I know I have to hang up. When I finally do, I cry most of the way back home.

Back in Shady Grove, I look at the video of Sara Meadows again. Yes, it definitely is something that Dylan Roberts should see. Then again, it could be a huge risk to send it to him. Keegan doesn't know that I have it. If he found out, what would he do? It's not like he can kill me. If he knew where I was, I'd be dead already.

Still, I have to trust somebody, and at least Dylan Roberts isn't on the force. He doesn't have ties to Keegan and his dirty cohorts. He didn't know my father, but he did know Brent. Maybe he would believe *him*, even if he doesn't believe me.

I go to the store and buy a thumb drive. I plug it in to my computer and copy all the information onto it, then I wipe it down to remove my fingerprints. I stop by work on the way home to grab a cardboard cell phone box. I'll use that to mail it to make it look like a cell phone is coming in the mail. If anybody is watching him hopefully they won't be suspicious.

I go home and create a business logo that looks professional, then I go by a Wi-Fi café and use their printer to print it out with a fake return address, then tape it onto the outside packaging. Then I drive up to Atlanta, since the postmark can't be from Shady Grove. I figure Dylan's already traced me to Atlanta anyway. I get there at midnight and drop it into an outgoing mailbox, hoping it will go out first thing in the morning. Then I head back to Shady Grove. It's two a.m. when I get there, and I'm tired, but sleep won't come. I lie awake in bed, staring at the ceiling, thinking about Brent. He's dead because of me, and now Sara Meadows is too. How could I have let that happen?

I should have kept the ghosts of my past to myself. I got too close to Brent, felt too comfortable. I drank wine with him one night over dinner, and my walls came down. I told him things I'd held close for years. I should have kept them buried.

His blood is on my hands. I'll never be able to get justice for myself or my dad, but at least I've learned something. I won't be that vulnerable again or put anyone else at risk. I won't let anyone else inside the blast zone of my ticking bomb. And I'll never let alcohol steal my judgment again.

I just hope I can stick to that plan. My love of people makes keeping a distance hard for me. It would be so much easier if I could stand being alone.

28

DYLAN

The explosion deafens me. The earth quakes, and a gust of hot wind knocks me back. I find myself crawling on all fours, searching for Tillis or Unger. I find Unger dead, his legs blown off. I scream for help, but no one comes. I see another IED planted just yards away, right where my commanding officer is running. I scream out *Nooooo!* and launch that direction to tackle him before he can reach it, but the distance grows longer and longer, and I can't quite close the gap between us. The bomb goes off and we both go flying.

I sit up suddenly, blasted by the air-conditioning in my dark bedroom. My heart beats wildly, and I'm drenched with sweat. Then I realize I'm not in my bed. I'm on the floor against the wall. My hands are bloody and shaking. It was another bad dream, a flashback to that day when it seemed everybody I knew was in bits and pieces, scattered over the Afghan terrain.

How did my hands get bloody? I look around. There's a broken glass shattered on the floor. I must've crawled through it. I will my hands to stop shaking as I get up and turn on the lamp. I pull the shards out, then try to clean the wounds.

I need to see my therapist as soon as daylight comes.

I watch TV, hoping to distract my brain from the terror. Andy Griffith plays for hours until the sun finally comes up. At eight o'clock I call Dr. Coggins. "Doc, this is Dylan Roberts. I need to see you," I say to her voice mail. "Please, can you get me in today? It's important."

I hang up, feeling unheard, but in fifteen minutes she calls me back. "Dylan, I can get you in at ten. Can you be here then?"

"Yes," I say. "Thank you."

I take a shower, washing off the dried blood, but I can't make my hands stop shaking. Sara Meadows' death has dragged me back in the wrong direction. Regression, Dr. Coggins will say. Maybe I should tell the Pace family that I can't continue this work. Maybe I can't continue any work, ever.

I go and sit in my therapist's office and tell her about the dream, about finding Sara Meadows dead, about my search for a murder suspect. She calms me down, as always, reads me

Scripture, prays over me. It's why I chose her, a shrink who believes in Christ and the spiritual warfare that goes on around me, adding to the memories of physical warfare still replaying in my brain. She understands the science of PTSD, but that's not all that matters to her. She makes me describe the worst hour of my life again, then two more times, forcing me to remember details. It's called cognitive repetition therapy, and it's designed to make my subconscious stop vomiting up the images in my sleep. If I can go there awake, maybe someday I won't have to go there in my dreams.

"You're making progress, Dylan," she says when we're almost done.

"How do you figure that?"

"You called me. You came here. You cooperated. You *want* to get better. That's a huge step."

I swallow hard. "I don't want to be disabled for the rest of my life. I'm thirty years old."

"You won't be. I know you can't see these incremental changes, but I do."

On our way out, I tell her I'm going to be traveling. "Call me if you need me," she says. "Make an appointment when you get back. Don't disappear on me, Dylan."

I hope I don't disappear on myself.

29

DYLAN

I sleep in the next day and watch an *Everybody Loves Raymond* marathon, useless and without purpose. My head aches and I have that oppressive, smothering feeling again that makes me want to end it all.

I spend most of the day arguing with myself, mentally citing reasons to live versus reasons I shouldn't. Then I spend hours hating myself for my self-pity.

I get my Bible and read the books of 1 and 2 Samuel and remember that my condition is not unique. When David escaped Saul's spears, he probably had a little PTSD himself. He managed to survive living in a cave while he dealt with that betrayal. He derailed his life a couple of times and always paid dearly, but he survived.

I can survive too.

By the time I reach the midnight hour, when life looks its most hopeless, I choose hope. I manage to sleep through the night.

In the morning, I decide that I'm worthless in this quest for Casey Cox. I don't know where she is, and every lead takes me to a dead end, or worse. Maybe I'll just quit.

At ten o'clock I go for a jog, forcing myself to run at least a mile. It will stimulate endorphins that I badly need. I drag myself around the neighborhood, sweating through my clothes, and can't wait to circle back to my apartment. The mailman is at the boxes when I get back, so I wait for him to leave, then check my own box.

Bills, junk mail, and one small box from some cell phone company. I haven't ordered anything, but it's definitely addressed to me.

I take it up to my apartment where *Everybody Loves Raymond* is still playing. I flick on the light and get a bottled water. As I'm drinking, I pick up the small package. I check the address again. It says it's from Atlanta and the postmark matches. I frown as I peel off the tape and open the box.

It's a thumb drive lodged between two wads of paper.

My breath catches. Could this be from Casey?

I grab my laptop from the kitchen counter, sink down on

my couch, and jab the thumb drive into the USB port. I finish off my water as the computer detects the new device and it shows up on the screen. I click on the thumb drive. There's a folder named "Cox Files."

Unbelievable. Who sent this? Sara Meadows before she died? No, she barely knew my name. Keegan? Maybe he finally answered my request. But he wouldn't have sent it from Atlanta. My heart trips. It has to be from Casey.

I click on it and see a list of files. Some are documents, some audio clips, and there's one video named "Sara Meadows."

I click on the video, wait as it loads, then it pops up on my screen. Ms. Meadows has on the blouse she was wearing in the video Keegan was watching yesterday. This must be the same video.

"This is Brent Pace." My heart stumbles as I hear my friend's voice. "I'm interviewing Sara Meadows, employed with the Shreveport Police Department. She was a clerk in the evidence room at the time of Andrew Cox's death—and still works there. Ms. Meadows, you said you were good friends with Officer Cox in the years leading up to his death."

My mouth falls open as I watch the video. She tells of the suspicions she had about some of the cops in the department. "There were some deaths when people fought back, and the findings of those homicides weren't consistent with the evidence logged. Andy was looking into some of the things these guys had bought with the money, paid cash for, and put under different names so they wouldn't be caught. After a couple of weeks, he came back to me, really shaken at what he'd found. Within three weeks, he was dead."

Brent asks her what I would have asked. "Did you tell anyone at the police department?"

"No, I was afraid. I thought they'd kill me too," she says. "But I made note of the evidence that came in, the stuff that was disregarded, like blood evidence from unidentified people. After the CSIs logged the evidence, the lead investigators determined what was relevant. The rest was pushed aside. It always worked out that they were the ones investigating these deaths."

Investigators on murder cases? *Detectives?* What is she saying? I listen as she goes on, then Brent asks her the same thing that's on my mind.

"Why would they have logged that as evidence if they were trying to cover it up?"

"The crime scene investigators logged it," Ms. Meadows says. "I think most of the CSIs are good guys. They did their jobs. I'm sure the killers had cleaned up the scenes as much as they could, but they couldn't hide everything. If the CSIs logged something that implicated the detectives, they just quashed it."

She describes how Casey found her father, and her thoughts on the kind of person who could leave that kind of scene for a twelve-year-old girl to find. Yes, she must have been traumatized—not to mention changed forever—by something like that.

"So you don't think the CSIs are involved?" Brent asks.

"I didn't until one of them was killed in a single-vehicle accident . . . just out of the blue. Other one retired and left the state."

"So let me get this straight," Brent says. "The detectives who covered up . . ."

"The only ones I know for sure are Gordon Keegan and Sy Rollins."

I lean back, both hands on my head. I stare at the video, stunned, unable to hear anything else.

Let's say she's right. If Keegan and Rollins are dirty, what does that mean? Did they manipulate the evidence in Brent's murder? Did they *kill* Brent? Did they kill Ms. Meadows?

I grab the remote and turn off the TV. Then I back up the video and force myself to focus.

She tells him she made a copy of the evidence logged in. Did she give it to Brent? I finish the video, then go back to the files and look for that evidence. Yes, there it is. The file named "Evidence Log."

So this is why Keegan didn't want to share the file with me. Too much didn't add up.

I feel the energy seeping back into my veins, my muscles, my bones. It's more than endorphins from running. It's purpose.

This doesn't tell me whether Casey killed Brent, but it does raise questions about his death. And her sending me the thumb drive tells me that she wants me to know the truth.

On the other hand, she's extremely smart. She could be manipulating me.

But no one I've talked to has called her manipulative. They've all been consistent in their love for her. And I talked to Sara Meadows myself. She was cautious . . . afraid . . . and she wanted to talk.

I feel sick that the old woman who made it this far with such a burning secret died for it in the end. Brent may have died for that same secret. Was Miss Sara killed because Keegan learned I'd spoken to her yesterday? Or did he decide to target her right after he saw the video? Was cancer taking too long to kill her?

It feels like I just crawled through the fallout of another IED. I have to be careful. Suddenly I feel paranoid. Someone might be listening to my calls, even to the things I say in my apartment. The paranoia doesn't feel like PTSD. It feels like realism. I have to get a message to Hannah with an e-mail address that Keegan isn't watching. It's imperative that I talk to Casey.

If all this is true, and Keegan and his cohorts are involved, then he doesn't want Casey to stand trial. He wants her dead. Isn't that what Hannah warned?

I have to get out of here. I decide to go back to Atlanta. Casey's most likely within driving distance of there, at least. I have to keep an open mind and proceed with caution. I still can't be sure she's not a psychopathic killer.

The psychopath is either my source or my target. I have to figure out which.

30

CASEY

Brent's thumb drive tucked into my sweaty palm, I count the days in my head and try to figure out if Dylan would have gotten it yet. What if he doesn't believe Brent's evidence? What if he turns it in to Keegan?

Fear leaves me paralyzed. What if sending it to him was the wrong thing? Thirteen years have gone by. Why would he believe me? Those corrupt cops got away with their crimes. They won. And now another person I loved is gone.

Since I can't control Dylan's reaction to the thumb drive, I force myself to switch my focus to checking out Frank Dotson and pursuing the lead on Laura Daly. But even in her case, I'm basically paralyzed. It's not like I can go to the police and get them to listen. All they'll say is that the man was probably interested in the case because she's a local girl who lived near him and that lots of women have cameo necklaces. Besides, I can't risk calling attention to myself.

I told you I was a coward. Still, I can't get it out of my mind. Finally, I find Frank Dotson's address on Google Maps and figure out that his house and the Dalys' are just two blocks apart. Maybe that *is* the reason Frank Dotson was hyperinterested in her case. But he stood there and lied to me. Wouldn't he have said, "Oh yeah, the family who lost that girl," if he didn't have something to hide?

I do a Google search on "Frank Dotson, Shady Grove, Georgia." Nothing comes up. I change "Frank" to "Francis." Several links appear on my screen.

Most are from People Search or Whitepages.com, but the fourth one that comes up is a paragraph from the police blotter that appeared in a Shady Grove newspaper.

Police were dispatched to the home of Francis Dotson, 185 Candrell Road, Sunday after a report of domestic violence. His wife, Arelle, reported injuries to her face and ribs. He was arrested and charged with assault and domestic abuse.

The report doesn't tell whether he was found guilty or served time, or if that marriage stayed intact. I scan the list for more articles or police blotters. I find another one, dated two years later. Again, his wife, Arelle Dotson, had reported a beating, and once again he was arrested.

So he has a violent history. I wonder if the police even considered him when Laura disappeared.

I decide to drive by his house. I change my appearance by tying a bandana on my head and wearing sunglasses. When I drive by the first time, I see a small house with grass that hasn't been mowed in some time. All the drapes and blinds are closed. There's no second story, but there does seem to be a basement.

I drive around the block until I'm directly behind the house and try to see through to the Dotsons' backyard. The back has a privacy fence, so I can't see much.

I drive by again, wishing I could catch someone outside. I know it would be ridiculous to think Laura would come bopping out, but maybe he does still have a wife. There was a woman in the pictures on his phone. I didn't see a divorce record in my search, but I'm not sure that I would. It looks as if nobody's home. There's no car in the single-bay carport.

As I drive away, I call Miss Lucy and shoot the breeze for a few minutes. Finally, I ask her what's on my mind. "Do you or Sandra know a guy named Frank Dotson?"

"I don't," Miss Lucy says. She puts her hand over the phone, and I hear her muffled voice asking Sandra. "Yes, she knows him," she says. "She says he lives around the block. Why, honey?"

"He came in the store a couple of days ago. I just wondered." I don't tell her that he claimed to not know their family.

"So have you found a place to live yet?" Miss Lucy asks.

"No, not yet, but I've made a few calls and I'm waiting for calls back."

"The offer is still open for you to rent Sandra's garage apartment. We'd love to have you."

The offer is tempting, but I will not pull Miss Lucy or Sandra into my mess. Even if I spend just one night there, that could make them accessories, harboring a fugitive. "Thanks, Miss Lucy. That's really sweet, but I need more room."

I don't really. I could easily live in a one-room apartment over someone's garage, but I prefer to rent from an apartment complex where no one is putting their life on the line by trusting me.

Someone beeps in, and I know it must be one of the landlords. I extract myself from the call and take it. There's an apartment available in my price range, not far from where I work. I tell the landlord I'll come look at it now.

Maybe on the way back I'll drive by Frank Dotson's house again.

31

CASEY

I look at the apartment and decide it'll do, so I put down a deposit and tell the landlord I'll move in immediately. I'll have to buy furniture, but I don't need much. A mattress, a chair, and a small TV will do. On my way home I drive past the Dotsons', park on the road perpendicular to their street, and watch their house for a while, hoping someone will come out. With its overgrown yard and peeling paint, the house looks like a condemned building in the midst of the neat little neighborhood, probably bringing property values down. Every window in the house has drapes closed, and the windows in the basement are boarded up.

I wonder why anyone would do that.

I'm getting ready to leave when the side door opens. I slide down in my seat as Frank and a woman come out. It's the woman from the pictures. Her hair is yellow, the color you get from bad at-home dye jobs. Dark roots are visible even from here, and not in a good way. I decide to see where they go. I stay down until they pass, then I turn around and follow them.

They lead me to a bar on West 36th Street in a seedy part of town that I didn't know was here. I guess every town has one. I don't feel like going in, so I sit there for a moment, waiting for them to come back out, but it could be a while. Then it occurs to me that I could go to their door while they're not home and see if I can hear anything in the house. The moment the thought occurs to me, the reasoning part of my brain screams out that it's ridiculous and risky. I'm already wanted for murder. Do I want to add trespassing to the mix?

But I can't stop thinking about Laura Daly. What if my hunch is right? What if she's really being hidden in that house somewhere, and no one's bothered to check? I could simply go to the door. That's not against the law, after all. So I get up my nerve and drive over there. I park across the street, walk up the cracked driveway, and step onto the porch. There's an old urn there with a dead plant that smells rank, as if the water has festered. I step around it, trying to see through the window, but it's covered.

I ring the bell. There's no sound of a dog barking or any-one's footsteps. Then I knock, loudly enough for anyone in the house to hear. When there's only silence, I walk to the side of the house, to the door I saw them coming out of, and I look at the basement window just above the ground, the window that's boarded up. I can't help myself. I stoop next to it and rap on the boards.

And I hear something.

A baby crying.

I catch my breath. Frank Dotson seems too old to have a child, and his wife doesn't look to be of childbearing age either. But I remember seeing a towheaded baby in his pictures. Maybe it's a grandchild, or they could have someone living with them. I quickly head back to my car, nervous that someone might look out and see me as I drive away.

On my way home, I call Sandra Daly at work. She picks up on the second ring. "Hey, Grace," she says. "What's up?"

"I just wanted to tell you I found a place to live," I say, trying to keep my voice upbeat. "I thought I'd check with you to make sure it's a good place."

"Oh, really? Where?"

I tell her, and she seems to think it's a decent choice. "I'm gonna move in tonight," I say. "I'm really excited about it." We chat about a couple more things, then I finally bring him up.

"Did your mother tell you that I ran in to one of your neighbors the other day?"

"Yeah," she says. "Frank Dotson, right?"

"Yes, do you know him well?"

"Well, not really, but he did help us search for Laura when

she went missing. He came to several of the volunteer days. I kind of got to know him that way. He seems like a nice guy. His neighbors wish he would mow his yard, though, maybe paint his house."

"Does he have children?" The question comes out of left field, and I hope it doesn't make her ask questions. Not yet anyway.

"I don't think so, but I guess it's possible. I have a friend who lives a couple of houses down from him. I can ask her. Why?"

I quickly try to come up with something. "I just had to go by his house to take something he left at the store, and nobody was home, or it didn't seem like they were. There was no car in the driveway and nobody came to the door. But I heard a baby crying. He seems too old to have a baby."

Sandra doesn't seem that interested. "Maybe it was the TV."

"Yeah, maybe. Sounded like a real baby, though. Would you ask your friend if there's a baby living in his home? A grandchild, maybe? I just don't like the feeling that a baby might have been left alone in there."

She laughs. "I'm sure he wouldn't leave a baby alone. Maybe he has houseguests who were afraid to answer the door."

"Yeah, maybe."

"I'll ask her, though."

I know she's wondering why I'm so interested. "Some things he said just kind of creeped me out."

Suddenly, Sandra gets quiet. "Grace, is this about Laura?"

I close my eyes. "No, no, not at all. I was just thinking there was something not right about him, and the thought of a baby living in his house . . ."

Sandra gets very quiet. Finally, I decide that I've done enough damage. "Look, I'm almost at Gran's Porch. I need to go. I've gotta pack up."

When she hangs up, I pull into the parking lot at the motel, turn off my car, and lean my head back on the seat. What am I doing? I must be crazy. The truth is, I'm probably much creepier than Frank Dotson. If Sandra knew she was dealing with a murder suspect, it would be me she feared, not him.

32

DYLAN

Dylan, my man!" Keegan's upbeat phone voice shakes me up. Has he heard I was at Sara Meadows' house when she was found? Will he wonder what I know? It chills me to know that he might've had something to do with all their deaths—Andy Cox's, Brent Pace's, and now Sara Meadows'—but I have to play it cool until I get the evidence I need.

"Hey," I say. "What's up?"

"I've got some news for you," he says. "We've traced the people accessing Brent Pace's friends' Facebook pages from out of town. Turns out there's someone who's accessed all of them from two places—Atlanta and Auburn, Alabama. We've traced them back to servers in public libraries in both of those areas, and we think it's probably Casey."

I wonder if he's blowing smoke, trying to send me on a wild-goose chase just to get me out of town and out of the way. But I have to consider that he might be telling the truth.

"Yeah, I know she was in Atlanta."

"She's somewhere within driving distance of those places. Smart girl. She probably wouldn't access their Facebook pages from wherever she's really hiding. Wherever it is, it's probably a couple of hours from both places."

"All right," I say. "I'll figure out the perimeters and see where they overlap."

"I need you to go there," Keegan says. "Go to the towns within that perimeter. Check to see if anybody's seen her."

If I trusted him, I'd ask why he hasn't sent press releases to every news outlet in Georgia and Alabama, but I think I know why. He wouldn't want another department to take her in. She might spill her guts, and the cops might listen.

A chill goes through me as I hang up. I get out a map, draw a circle with a radius of 150 miles from Auburn, another 150 miles from Atlanta, then I study the area where they intersect.

I decide to drive over in my own car, and I'll stop at every police department in every town and every post office in that intersecting perimeter, showing Casey's picture to see if anyone recognizes her. Since I doubt that I'll sleep tonight anyway, I pack my car and head out. I'll be there by morning.

33

CASEY

The next day off I have, I drive across the Alabama state line to call my sister again. Since I texted her to warn her, she's ready for me this time, waiting without her baby, far from her car or anything that might be wired. I can hear the wind. She must be outside again.

"What did you do with the information I gave you about Dylan Roberts?" she asks. "Did you contact him?"

I pause for a moment. "I'd rather not tell you anything," I say. "If they interrogate you again, the less you know, the better."

"Okay, but I hope you did," she says. "The more I've thought about it, the more I think it's the right thing to do."

"Can we change the subject?" I ask.

"Sure," she says. "What is it?"

"I've got a problem," I say.

She laughs. "Besides being wanted for murder and having the real killers hunting you down?"

It's not funny. I don't know what to say.

"Sorry," she says. "Tell me what's going on."

I sigh and tell her about Miss Lucy and how I met her. "So this woman has a granddaughter who's missing. She's been missing for two years. She's sixteen now, if she's still alive."

"That's awful."

"There's no sign of her," I tell Hannah. "There has never been a clue of what happened or where she might be. Only now I think I might know."

Hannah sucks in a breath. "What do you mean, you think you might know?"

"Well, there's this guy who came in the other day to where I work. He left his cell phone, and I looked at his photos. His wife had a necklace like Laura's, and they had all these newspaper clippings of her."

"The girl who went missing?"

"Yes," I say. "It just gave me a creepy feeling. I mean, why would he save all that?"

"Casey, you need to stay out of this. You have your own problems. You shouldn't be snooping through a man's pictures."

"I know, but there's a girl missing. Her life is at stake. Her family mourns her every single day."

"What did you do?" she asks, as if she already knows the answer and doesn't like it.

I sigh. "Well, I went and knocked on the door when I knew he wasn't home, just to see what I could hear."

"You went to his door? Are you insane?"

"Just listen. I heard a baby crying."

"A baby? I thought you said she was sixteen."

"Remember those other girls who went missing and had babies? The ones in Ohio . . . and Jaycee Dugard? Maybe Laura's had a baby too."

"Casey, you're jumping to conclusions! You need to stop this."

I know she's right.

Her voice has faded into a theatrical whisper. "If anybody sees you trespassing on his property, they're going to call the police, and what happens if they print you and find out that you're wanted for murder in Shreveport? This is dangerous!"

"I know," I say, tears pushing to my eyes. I bring my hand to my mouth.

"Casey, I'm trying to help you. Listen to me. If you're going to be that reckless, then you might as well just come home. All this is wasted if you wind up getting caught and killed anyway."

I'm quiet for a moment. When I speak again, my voice is

raspy. "It's just . . . if I can't be a hero in my own life, maybe I can be one in someone else's."

I can tell Hannah's crying now. Her breathing sounds wet. "Casey, I know your heart goes out to this girl. I know you always want to help everybody, but if it's true . . . if this guy is the one who kidnapped her . . . if he's holding her in his basement, then he's dangerous. I don't want to know that you're doing something so scary."

"I'm not doing anything scary," I say. "But if I don't stand up for her, who will?"

"Go to the police!" she says.

"The police?" I ask. "You know I can't do that."

"Casey, not every cop in every town is dirty. We can't think like that. The odds are that the ones there are honest, like Dad. The kind of people who get up every morning and know they're putting their lives on the line. The kind who risk getting shot every time they pull someone over. The kind who do it anyway because they believe in justice."

"I know that's true. Most of them are good. But the corrupt ones seem so powerful."

"You could send the local police an anonymous tip about the girl. Send them the evidence you have. They could look into it, then you don't have to do anything else. For all you know, they might have already thought of this person and they might have a case file on him. This might be just what they need to push them into getting a search warrant."

"He's their neighbor," I say. "I mean, if I were a cop, I would've already looked at all the neighbors. Right?"

"Maybe."

"Laura's mother says this man helped in the search. Dad used to say that happens a lot. The perpetrator often gets involved in the case. It's a power trip for a sociopath."

"But don't you think the police know that? Don't you think they checked on everybody who joined the search?"

"Probably."

"So send them what you have anonymously. You don't have to tell them anything else. Just tell them that you know for a fact that he's collecting articles about Laura Daly and has that necklace, that you saw a picture and then you saw the articles, and that you've heard a baby crying in his house."

"I'll think about it," I say.

"Don't just think about it, Casey. You can't be a hero here. You're going to get killed. Do I need to remind you that if they find you, it's not just about prison? They want you dead. I don't want to lose another family member. I feel like I've already lost you."

"You haven't lost me," I say. "I'm still here."

"You won't be if you do this. I'll just stop getting calls from you one day, and I won't know"—her voice catches—"Casey, I'm sorry about that girl, but there are other ways that you can help her, ways that don't involve the police talking to you."

When I hang up, I have to admit that part of my struggle

is that I don't *want* to do it. I'm a coward. That's why I haven't gone back to Shreveport and fought this charge. That's why I haven't told my side of the story to everyone. I don't want to be locked up, and I don't want to die.

I also don't want another girl to be locked up, and now there may be a baby involved. The thought of it overwhelms me. As I drive home, I wish I had what it takes to save someone. Anyone. Even if it's not me.

34

CASEY

Despite my sister's cautions to stay out of the Laura Daly case, I try every way I know to find out if Frank Dotson has any children or grandchildren who might've been in the house the day I knocked on the door. I realize I could be jumping to conclusions—no, not jumping, taking giant leaps. Just because I heard a baby doesn't mean that he has Laura.

But one afternoon at work, my coworker Rachel mentions hanging out at the bar where I saw Dotson and his wife go.

"How often do you go there?" I ask.

She shrugs. "Two, three times a week. It's just where my friends hang out. You should come sometime."

"Maybe I will." I try not to look too interested. "Do you know Frank Dotson and his wife?"

She nods as she opens the back of a phone to change out its battery. "Yeah, I know Frank. He's a regular."

"What kind of person is he?"

She looks up at me. "I don't know. Keeps to himself, I guess. Why? You interested?"

"Um, no." I chuckle. "I don't know. He came in here the other day. Just seemed a little creepy."

She laughs. "Yeah, creepy's a good word. His wife is creepier. Sticks to him like glue, does everything he says, drinks a lot."

"Do they have children?" I ask.

She shakes her head. "No, never had any. I don't think they're the parenting type."

"So no grandkids . . . ?"

She laughs. "It's hard to have grandkids when you don't have kids."

I have to give her that one. "So how long have they been married?"

"As long as I've known them," she says. "But like I said, I don't know them all that well. They're big, heavy drinkers, and they fight a lot."

I look at her. "In public?"

"Yeah, sometimes when Arelle gets a little too drunk, she starts mouthing off to him. He usually jerks her up and drags her out. I wouldn't be surprised if there was a little domestic abuse going on in that situation."

I watch as she tosses the old battery. "Have you ever seen him be violent?" I ask.

"No, I haven't seen it, but she's come in with a black eye before, claimed she fell."

"Has anyone ever intervened? At the bar, I mean."

"No. He's usually just cussing at her and trying to get her out the door so she'll shut up."

"What kind of stuff does she say when she's mouthing off?"

"Who knows? You can hardly ever understand her. The last time it was about his eyes roaming and him flirting with a girl in the bar. Come to think of it, that's always what it's about. His wandering eyes."

The thought makes me shudder. A customer comes in and I wait on her. When she's gone, I turn back to Rachel. "Has that guy Frank ever come on to you?"

"Gross. No, I've never gotten that close to him. Has he hit on you? Is that why you're asking?"

I evade the question as she waits on the next customer.

That afternoon as I drive home from work, I consider what I've learned. There is no offspring in that house, no baby to cry, no grandchild. So what does that mean? What I heard could have been a television, but it didn't sound like one. For a moment I consider going to the police, telling them what I heard, what I saw in the pictures, asking them to do a welfare check to make sure there's no baby there. *And oh yes, while you're there, look to see if that missing girl Laura Daly is in there.*

But then I realize how crazy that would sound without any

evidence. A newspaper article in the background of a picture, a necklace that anyone might have, the sound of a baby crying when I knocked on the boarded window. It wouldn't convince anyone of anything, especially when Laura Daly isn't known to have had a baby. And it might just call unnecessary attention to me—the trespasser, the one whose curiosity could get her killed.

I have to decide whether to help Laura or myself. It probably can't be both.

35

CASEY

The choice should be easy. I should simply do what's right and try to rescue Laura. But being wanted for murder creates a delicate balance in my universe. Tipping to either side, even the slightest bit, could result in my being caught.

At first I convince myself that it's not cowardly to ignore my gut on this. It's survival. Giving up my ability to survive in order to rescue Laura, when I could be entirely wrong about her being in that house, is not wise.

Instead of spending time watching Frank Dotson's house, I should be digging up all the evidence I need to make my case back home, so I can save myself when the time comes. I should be digging into Keegan's and Rollins's financial situations, proving they're criminals masquerading as cops, proving that they killed my father and made it look like suicide, proving that they murdered Brent and set me up. I should be trying to figure out who else is in it with them.

But I've tried over the years to prove those things and have gotten nowhere. To expose them, I have to risk being found.

The idea of suicide surfaces again, but I quickly banish it. I don't want anyone to say, "There, I told you those Coxes were suicidal. It's in their blood. Like father, like daughter." No, they're never going to have more reason to believe my dad took his own life and left his twelve-year-old daughter to find him.

But if they find me and drag me back to Shreveport, death is inevitable anyway. I'll never have the chance to talk.

Loneliness is a side effect of my reality. I need to talk to Hannah, just to tamp that loneliness a little. Though I'm tired and want to watch the Dotson house again tonight, I drive two hours out of town. I buy another disposable phone, activate it, and call my sister. I let it ring twice, long enough to register a "missed call." Then I give her an hour to get away from any possible bugs in her house or car. I know this could all be for naught, because she has a child and a husband and can't just leave whenever she wants. But when I call back, she answers.

"Hey," she says.

"Where are you?" I ask.

"In the parking lot of Walgreens. I didn't want to go anywhere after dark that wasn't lit up."

"Good. I'm sorry to get you out at night."

"Are you all right?" she asks.

"Yes. I just wanted to hear your voice."

"I'm glad you called," she says. "Listen, I have a message for you."

I draw a breath. "From who?"

"From Dylan Roberts."

My heart jerks. "Hannah, you haven't admitted we talk have you?"

"No, but if you sent him the thumb drive, it's pretty obvious. Just listen. He sent a note to my in-laws' house. The return address was another sporting goods place in Seattle, just like your package to me."

I sigh. "Did they open it?"

"No, they think it's something else for Jeff's birthday."

"What does the note say?"

"It says, 'Tell her to create a dummy e-mail address and contact me at this address. Urgent. My eyes are opening.'"

She reads out his e-mail address, and I write it down. "So you think I should risk contacting him?"

"You're smart. Do what you're doing with me. Drive out of town. Go to a library and get online. Create an e-mail address. If it's traced, it'll be traced to the library, not to you."

"What about him? How do I know *he's* being smart? They could be watching him and intercept my e-mail."

"I think he's too smart for that. He knows how things work," she says. "I think you should do it. I want you to know what he knows."

"I'll think about it," I say. There's a long pause, and I hear the wind on the line. I picture my sister standing in the parking lot at night alone. "You need to get back home."

"Wait," she says. "You haven't done anything about that girl Laura, have you?"

"No. Not yet."

"I'm begging you to stay off the radar," she says. "Don't mess this up trying to rescue someone else. It's not worth it."

I know my sister means well with those words, but as I drive back to Shady Grove, I have a lot of time to think. Laura Daly's life isn't worth my risk? If I'm the only one who has an inkling of where she might be, how dare I put it out of my mind? Now there might be two lives, instead of just one. Laura and a baby. What if they really are there?

I have trouble sleeping when I get back to my new apartment. I give up around four in the morning and get up and look out the window into the dark. The streetlight in front of my building is flickering, indecisive about whether to provide a safe glow for the road or snuff itself out entirely.

I don't want to be snuffed out. I look up at the night sky, stars flickering. I ask God if I still have a function. Or have all my lies robbed me of my soul? Am I just a liar with a fake ID? Or does God see me as a living, breathing, compassionate girl who cares about Laura Daly?

For someone who doesn't know if she believes in God, I'm sure aware of him a lot. I recognize that irony.

As the sun blanches the darkness from the sky, slowly brightening into day, I make my decision. I will save Laura Daly if I can, no matter what it means for me.

36

DYLAN

As I consider reporting Keegan and Rollins with the evidence Brent collected, I realize that if I do, I'll be painted as paranoid and incompetent, the damaged vet who jumps at every noise. Sara Meadows' testimony is largely speculative, not enough to conclusively nail Keegan, and the DA would give him the benefit of the doubt since cops are usually the good guys. I can't do it. Not yet.

I have to be systematic. I start with what Brent gathered and dig deeper. I have to link the men to the other murders, find the money they've extorted, record the things they've bought with that money. I have to consider the possibility that Sara Meadows might have had dementia. But no, that doesn't make sense. Why would she have wound up dead if her accusations were delusional?

My brain likes patterns, things lined up nice and orderly. Something about this case hasn't added up from day one. Casey doesn't fit the pattern of a murderer. Nothing about her suggests she could kill. But now that I've seen Brent's files, the Keegan theory clicks into place. That's a pattern that makes more sense than an otherwise decent girl suddenly cracking up.

But can I even trust myself? Doubts crest like vultures in my mind, circling my theories, swooping to feed on them. They make me second-guess my competence, my objectivity, my skills. What if I'm just being conned?

I'm not, I tell myself. I'm following the evidence. I'm doing what I was trained to do. But my self-talk doesn't help. I need to talk to my shrink.

On the way to Georgia, I call Dr. Coggins.

She answers, and the sound of her voice reminds me it's the middle of the night. "I'm so sorry to wake you," I say. "I didn't realize how late it is."

I hear her bed rustling, her husband's voice, then she comes across more clearly. "What is it, Dylan?"

I suddenly can't think of what I wanted to say. I can't tell her all that's happened. "I should've waited till morning."

"You've gotten me up now," she says. "Dylan, tell me what's going on."

I feel like a fool. "You know how I told you I'm doing some PI work?"

"Yes."

"Well, I'm at a crossroad. I just got some information that flips everything around. I feel like the bad guy is really the good guy, and the supposedly good guy is really bad. Only I still have a job to do . . . to find this person who may be vicious, but is probably good."

I know I'm not making sense. I sound like I'm drunk or high.

"Dylan," she says. "Sometimes feelings aren't the best things to go on, especially when you're dealing with PTSD. When you had that nightmare and cut up your hands, you *felt* like you were back there, living through it again. But you were wrong."

I consider that. "But this isn't the PTSD. This is real."

"Dylan, you don't want to lose this opportunity. My advice is to finish the job you were hired to do. Stay the course. Don't be swayed by feelings. Just practice what you know."

I know police work, and I know I'm close to finding Casey. If I can just apprehend her, then maybe I can keep her safe while I sort out the truth from the lies. "You're right," I say.

She's quiet for a moment, then says, "You sure you don't want me to write you a prescription for something to help you sleep?"

I figure she probably wants me sleeping so I won't call her in the middle of the night. "No thanks, Doc. Maybe later . . ."

I resign myself to staying on track and finding Casey.

I've e-mailed Casey's picture and the charges against her to every police and sheriff's department in Georgia, asking them to contact me if they've seen her, but the truth is, they get dozens of these a week. In the smaller departments, they may not check their e-mail for days.

There are 536 municipalities in Georgia. It's impossible to hit every one of them. As day breaks, I try to think like Casey, getting off at the towns along I-75 to visit libraries and post offices and stopping by police departments, just to make sure they saw my e-mail.

No one has seen her.

And my assumptions may be all wrong anyway. She may not be in Georgia at all. She could be in Florida or South Carolina . . . or almost anywhere.

What do I know for sure? I know that she got on Facebook from some server in Auburn, Alabama, at least twice, so wherever she is, she's within driving distance of that town. She's probably not in Alabama, because she has family there, and she would know we'd look there. East central Georgia is as good a place to start as any.

At Barnesville, I walk into the small police station populated by three people. The Barnesville sheriff's department hasn't seen the e-mail, so I show them Casey's picture and tell them that she's going under the alias of Grace Newland. They do a quick search through recent arrest records. No one present has seen her, and they want to know what she's done. I tell them she's a murder suspect in Shreveport, that it's very important that they call me if they get any clue as to where she might be. They ask me if she's armed and dangerous.

I tell them I don't know, that they should assume she is until they find out otherwise.

Driving away from Barnesville, I wonder if I've done the wrong thing. That statement alone could get her killed by some half-cocked deputy who wants to make a name for himself.

When the post office and librarians say they haven't seen her, I shake the dust off my feet and go to the next town. I figure I'll start with the towns along the interstate, and once I exhaust those, I'll branch out, taking smaller roads. This could be a long process. I stop at each town along the way, leaving info about Casey.

Fatigue pulls at my body, and weird ideas work on my brain. It's like she's a phantom, like she doesn't even exist. How could she always be a few steps ahead of me, unable to be tracked? This hasn't happened to me before. I can usually find clues, disassemble carefully constructed plans, get into the head of the person I'm looking for. But Casey's not the typical criminal.

I realize that she's growing larger in my mind, taking on mythical powers and insight. She's human, I remind myself. She can't have thought of everything. I finally check into a motel and try to sleep, but fail again. After a while, I go into the business office where the computers are. Instead of using my own laptop, I get on theirs, open up the new e-mail account I've created, and check to see if she's contacted me.

I'm shocked to see that she has. The e-mail handle she's used is NotGoingDown. I quickly click on it, open the message.

"Here I am," she wrote. "What do you want?"

My breath catches in my chest. I whisper a quick prayer— *Please, Jesus!*—and start to type.

"I read and viewed everything you sent me from Brent's package," I type. "I found Sara Meadows and I went to talk to her. She told me to come to her house that night, that she had some things to say, but when I got there, she was dead."

I start a new paragraph as sweat prickles my skin.

"I have to consider that maybe what Brent found was true. That puts me in a hard position."

I wipe my hands on my jeans and place them on the keyboard again. I can't think what to say. I have to appeal to her, one human to another. This might be my only chance, so I open my heart and try to be honest.

"I think you and I have a lot in common. We both have PTSD. You can't look into the eyes of a dead human being, someone you loved, and not have your soul changed. I believe in God, and it feels like he's telling me to listen to you. But I need more hard evidence. I don't blame you for hiding, but maybe it's time to come back. Maybe it's time to get the truth out. Maybe I can help you."

I don't know why my heart is racing like I've run five miles, or why my eyes are watering like I'm running into the wind. "Do you have nightmares?" I type.

"Do you startle easily? Do you have crazy reactions to

things that shouldn't cause such a response? Do you some-times think you're going crazy? I do. And if you found your dad murdered when you were twelve years old, I bet you do. Your experiences with the police have driven you further away, rather than given you faith that justice will be served. I can't promise you that it will be, but I'll do whatever is in my power."

I lean back and wipe my damp face, check the door. No one lurks in the hall.

Hands back on the keyboard, I type, "Tell me what I need to know. Give me facts that can be verified. And if you can call me, I have a burner phone that no one has access to. The number is 318-555-2753. Memorize it so you can use it when the time is right."

I don't sign my name. I leave it blank, as if I don't know who I am anymore. But *she* knows.

Before I hit Send, I press my face into my hands and say a silent prayer that God will sort this out, that he'll get the e-mail to her, that she'll see it quickly, that we can get a good correspondence going, and that the Holy Spirit will lead me into discernment and truth.

I wait a few minutes, hoping she'll write back immediately, but I know better than that. She's not going to check on her own phone or computer. She'll drive across state lines, use a library computer. It could take days before I hear again.

I close out of that window, get the computer back to the login screen, and go back to my room. I try to sleep, but it continues to evade me.

I take shallow catnaps during the night, hoping it's enough to keep me from being a zombie the next day. Before I leave, I check the computer downstairs again. She hasn't responded, but she will. She wouldn't have contacted me, risking exposure, if she didn't have something to say. As I drive out of town, I find myself praying for her protection, her strength, and her courage to tell the truth. And I pray that I'll find her before Keegan does.

37

CASEY

watch the Dotsons' house again, waiting for Frank and Arelle to leave. For several nights they stay indoors, not showing their faces. Since I have to work I can only come at night, but I can't stop myself. It's like an obsession.

By Saturday, I'm exhausted, but I still can't sleep. I can't even eat. I chew food, knowing I need fuel, but somehow I'm too tired to swallow it. I force myself nonetheless.

I drive three hours down to Mobile to see if I got an e-mail from him. I get to a library that smells of mildew and dust. The computers are right out in the open, around the edges of a big round table. People sit there for hours on Facebook, wasting time. I have to wait for an opening, and after an hour, someone finally leaves. I get their place and sign in to my e-mail with my NotGoingDown alias. There's an answer in my inbox.

I shiver as I read the message, and I look around to make sure no one is reading over my shoulder. I zoom out on the screen so the font is smaller.

"I think you and I have a lot in common. We both have PTSD. You can't look into the eyes of a dead human being, someone you loved, and not have your soul changed. I believe in God, and it feels like he's telling me to listen to you . . .

"Do you have nightmares? Do you startle easily? Do you have crazy reactions to things that shouldn't cause such a response? Do you sometimes think you're going crazy? I do. And if you found your dad murdered when you were twelve years old . . ."

His words make me sweat. It's as if he's peeked into my psyche and seen those videotapes that play so often in my head.

Murdered. He said *murdered*, not suicide. He believes Brent. He isn't yet convinced of *my* innocence, but he is beginning to at least consider that Keegan is dirty.

Or is it an act? For all I know, this could be Keegan himself.

I press Reply, then type, "No, I don't sleep much. Nightmares are painful bedfellows. And you're right about my not trusting justice. I'm glad you believe in God. I hope that brings you comfort."

I try to think of something I can tell him, some morsel of truth that, even if I'm talking to Keegan, will penetrate.

"There is real evil in this world," I type. "I've seen it up close. Hiding for the rest of my life would be an acceptable cost for avoiding that evil. If only it weren't everywhere."

I pause for a moment, wishing I were more prepared.

"I've given you everything I have. Do you have the courage to go after the evil that plagues me, even if it means that the job you've been hired to do is an extension of that evil?"

Tears come to my eyes, but I blink them back.

"Here are the names. Keegan, Sy Rollins, for sure. Don't trust their close friends or Keegan's son. Keegan and Rollins are not just dirty, they are brutal. Evil sits in the Major Crimes Unit, making proclamations on people like me."

That's all I dare say. I send the e-mail and hurry back to my car. I feel like Dylan has read some journal that I haven't even written. How does he know those things about me? Facts are one thing, but *truth* goes deeper. It cuts to the heart. He can't possibly know what's in my head.

Yet he nailed it.

I wonder about the nature of his PTSD. Was he diagnosed, or is he like me . . . struggling with the aftermath without giving that struggle a name? His words about looking into the eyes of the dead . . . they haunt me. He knows.

I feel exposed . . . violated, in a way. But also validated. In some ways, it's good to be *seen*, even if he's never laid eyes on me.

When I reach Shady Grove, I don't want to go home. I

know I'm too wired to sleep tonight, and I don't want to stare at my ceiling and think.

I go to my latest hangout—the shadowy places on Frank Dotson's street. Evil sits in that house too. At least maybe I can do something about that.

After two hours of no activity, I see the lights of their car coming on. They're coming out. As they get into their car and pull out of their driveway, I use my binoculars to see if the woman is in the car with him. Yes, his wife is sitting there, her angular features a silhouette against the streetlight. Once again I follow them to the bar.

This is my chance.

I can go back to their house and walk around back, see if all those basement windows are boarded up.

I go to Home Depot just before it closes. I buy a crowbar, two screwdrivers, and a flashlight. I have a backpack in my trunk, which I get out when I return to my car. I shove my purchases into it and put it on my passenger seat.

I sit in my car for a moment, staring at the windshield. Am I really contemplating breaking and entering? No, I tell myself. Just breaking and rescuing. But even as I consider it, I know how crazy that will sound if I'm caught.

But I challenged Dylan to have the courage to go after evil. I have to be willing to do it myself. That's the kind of person I want to be. There's a life at stake—probably two—and if I can just get evidence that they're in there, it could save them. I have to do it.

I head back to the Dotson house. My heart thumps as I park my car at the curb a few houses down between yards, so that neither resident will think I'm at their house. I walk in the darkness back to the Dotsons'.

I slip through the gate into the backyard and shine my flashlight. The two other basement windows are boarded up from the outside. Why would anyone do that, unless they didn't want someone to get out? I go back to the window where I heard the baby. There's a broken patio in front of it, and I almost trip over the cracked brick pavers. I get down on my knees and look for the screws in the board covering the window. It takes a while, but I get the first screw out, then I locate four others. I work slowly, steadily, sweat dripping into my eyes. The light in the backyard next door comes on, and I freeze for a moment and watch to see if anyone is looking over the fence. When it stays quiet, I keep working, but I get impatient by the time I get to the last two screws. My wrist is hurting, and I'm not moving fast enough. Frank and his wife could come home and then I'd lose this chance. So I use the crowbar and pry the board off the last two screws. It creaks and cracks, and I glance back at the neighbor's light. I still don't see anyone, so I keep going.

On the inside of the glass there's another board. Who would board their basement windows from the inside *and* the outside? It doesn't even make sense, unless they're trying to keep someone trapped in there.

I bang hard on the glass, listening. There it is. The crying baby again, as if I've startled it. It's *not* the TV. This is a real baby. I'm not going to leave here without knowing who's in that basement.

I know that if I break the glass, one of the neighbors might hear, but I can't seem to stop myself. I get the crowbar, tap the glass. It makes too much noise, but the glass cracks. I tap it again and it shatters. I pull away the shards, cutting my hand, but I keep going. When I get to the board on the other side, I bang again.

"Is anybody there? Can you hear me?"

Suddenly, there's a tap, then a girl's voice. It sounds distant, far away. "Help me!" she cries.

My heart jolts. "I'm trying!" I say. "Who are you?"

"Laura," she says. "Laura Daly."

The name shatters me. I force myself to get a grip. I sit back on the dirt and kick with both feet, trying to break through the board. When I can't budge it, I look around. There's a cellar door that I didn't notice before, between the two windows. I try to throw it open, but it's locked. If only I had bolt cutters.

I go back to the window with my crowbar and jam it against the casing. "Hold on," I say as loudly as I dare. "I'm coming to get you. Just wait!"

The baby keeps screaming, but I can tell that they're closer, waiting at the window for their escape. I whisper a prayer while I work. "I know you don't know me, and I don't know you. But you know Sandra and Miss Lucy, and they trust you."

I kick again and again, trying to crack the boards loose, but it's screwed too tight. I wedge the crowbar in, hoping to splinter the board. If I just have enough time, I know I can get through.

"Freeze!"

Lights flood all around me, blinding me. I drop back on my haunches, hands in the air.

"Drop your weapons!"

"I don't have any weapons," I say.

"Drop it!"

I'm surrounded. I've done it now. I drop the crowbar. Someone grabs me, throws me down. My ear grinds into the dirt. As they cuff me, I shout, "It's Laura Daly! She's in the basement. I talked to her. She told me—!"

No one's listening. They drag me to the car, my hand dripping with blood where I cut it. They shove me into the backseat.

I tell them again when they get me to the police station. They pull my driver's license out of my purse, which they've retrieved from my car. I wonder where my car is now. Did they drive it here or did they leave it on the Dotsons' street? I wonder if they'll realize that Grace Newland doesn't exist, that she's a dead girl and I've stolen her identity.

This is the worst that could happen, I think. Then I correct myself. The worst that could happen is that Laura Daly is never found, that Frank Dotson keeps her trapped in that basement. The worst that could happen is that she had a little hope only to have it dashed. When they tell Frank Dotson that his house was broken into, he could kill her just to dispose of the evidence.

I've got to get out of here, if only to stop that. "I'm telling you," I say in a quivering voice. "Laura Daly, the girl who's been missing for two years, is in that house. Why won't you listen?"

"If that's true, why didn't you call the police?" the detective asks me.

"Because the police never listen," I say. "This is the perfect example. I'm the person trying to rescue her, and I'm sitting in handcuffs instead of him! Will you at least go check? Get a search warrant. Go in his house. I'm telling you, she's there in the basement. She has a baby. I talked to her!"

"She told you she was Laura Daly?"

"Yes! How many times do I have to tell you? Please," I say. "What if I'm telling the truth? You could save a girl's life!"

They keep questioning me about who I am, where I came from, and I try to remember the details I memorized about Grace Newland. I tell them I work at the cell repair store, where I live, that I know Miss Lucy and Sandra Daly. I try to get them off the subject of my identity, but they keep questioning me about how many houses I've broken in to lately, what I was trying to get, where I'm keeping the stolen goods. I know it's just a matter of time before they realize I'm not who I say I am, that I'm really Casey Cox, wanted for murder in Shreveport, Louisiana. That I'm not a petty thief. I'm a fugitive, on the run and hiding.

Finally, they book me, and I see a judge who sets my bond. I have to come up with a thousand dollars. I use my one phone call to call Miss Lucy. Instead of telling her I'm under arrest, I start with the most important thing. "I know where Laura is," I say.

Miss Lucy sucks in a breath. *"What?"*

"I found her," I say. "She's in Frank Dotson's basement. I think she has a baby."

Miss Lucy is frozen in silence. Seconds pass. "Did you tell the police?"

"Yes, but I got arrested trying to break in to help her, and I'm in jail."

"Casey!"

"I need your help," I cry. "I need you to post bond for me. A thousand dollars. I have it. I'll pay you back the minute I get out."

"Honey! Of course I will, but . . . you told the police about Laura?"

"Yes, but they won't listen. You have to make them. She's alive!"

I hear her voice break as sobs rise up. "Oh, dear God, could it be?"

"It *is*! I promise, Miss Lucy." My words rattle rapid-fire. "He's going to do something to her. He can't let them find her. He'll be desperate now that he knows someone is on to him."

I hear her talking to Sandra, her voice muffled. "Casey, we'll be there in a few minutes."

I know I can count on it. I hang up the phone and look down at my cut hand.

"You need stitches," the trustee behind the counter says.

"I don't care about that," I whisper.

She disappears into a back room and comes out with a first-aid kit. "Here, you need a bandage, at least. Are they bailing you out?"

"Yes."

"Then get them to take you to a hospital."

"No," I say. "I'm fine. The bandage will be enough. It's not a deep cut."

She wraps my hand, and the small kindness makes me burst into tears.

As I wait for Miss Lucy and Sandra, I realize I have a lot to be thankful for. Apparently the local police haven't searched deeply enough into my identity to find out that the girl I purport to be is actually dead. Maybe it's a big burglary night, and they just haven't had time. Now that they know I'm here in Shady Grove, I have to leave. But I can't leave Laura to die. If they don't find her, I have to go back, even if it means I get caught. Even if it means I go down for murder. Even if it means I die.

38

CASEY

'm waiting in my car at Sandra's and Miss Lucy's when they
get home. They've been sitting in a police cruiser, watching as
police search the Dotson house. I've been waiting here, practically unable to breathe.

But I know the minute they get out of their car that they
have bad news. Sandra bursts into tears when she sees me.

I get out and walk toward them. "Didn't they find her?"

"No." She looks so forlorn that it breaks my heart.

"Well, did they look in the basement?"

Miss Lucy's eyes are red and swollen, but she's holding it

together now. "They searched everywhere. There was no baby and no Laura. They questioned his wife, who they said is mentally ill. Maybe it was her you heard."

"No, she was with *him*! She was at the bar with her husband. They can confirm that. It wasn't her I talked to. It was Laura. She told me so!"

"She wasn't there, Grace."

Sandra sounds irritated with me, and I don't blame her. To get her hopes up like that, to think once again that she might have her daughter back, only to be disappointed . . .

But I know what I heard. "He moved her, then. He knew they were going to come. After the police took me . . . before the search warrant . . . Just because she wasn't there when they searched doesn't mean she never was."

She's looking at me now as if I'm the one who's mentally ill, and I know she's questioning what voices I might hear in my head. I feel sick. They're never going to believe me. Laura's never going to be rescued.

"Sandra, I'm not making this up."

"What good does it do if I believe you?" Sandra asks. "It doesn't make any difference at all!" She runs into her house, but Miss Lucy stays outside.

"Come here," she says.

I go into her arms. She feels like my mom used to feel, before she fell apart. I weep against her shoulder, and she weeps against mine.

"I'm so sorry," I say through my sobs. "But I know she

was there. I can't explain why they didn't find her, but she was there."

"I believe you, sweetheart," Miss Lucy says. "I know you meant well."

The second sentence negates the first. I pull away from her, wipe my face and my nose. I just want to go home. I want to crawl into bed and bury myself under the covers. I want to cry alone.

I want to give this family some peace, if that's even possible.

I walk away, leaving Miss Lucy in the driveway. "Honey, are you going to be all right?" she asks.

"I'm fine," I say as I get in my car.

"You won't do anything dangerous, will you?"

I don't answer her. I just get in, lock my doors, and drive home. When I get to my apartment, I don't even bother to turn on the lights. I drop my purse and keys on the floor and climb in bed, clothes and all. I don't care if I never see daylight again.

39

DYLAN

Keegan's phone call comes as I'm merging off I-75 onto Highway 280. I hope my disgust for him doesn't show in my voice.

"Guess what I just found out," Keegan says, his voice gleeful. "Casey's alias—Grace Newland—is really the name of a dead girl who lived in Oklahoma City and died two years ago. So it occurs to me . . . What if Casey had something to do with *her* death?"

"She didn't," I say. "I've already looked into that. The death certificate said she died of natural causes. Her family still has a Facebook page up for her. I went back to the time of her death. It was cancer. There are pictures of her without hair, in the hospital, fighting for her life."

Keegan sounds disappointed. "Well, guess you're a step ahead of me."

I can tell he doesn't like it a bit. "It wasn't that hard," I say, then quickly add, "You have a lot more to do than I do."

When I hang up, I pray he will stay a few steps behind until I can find Casey.

I've sent out a second e-mail to every sheriff's department and police department in Georgia, along with her picture, asking if they've seen this girl going by the name of Grace Newland. So far, I've gotten only negative responses. No one who's replied has seen her.

I finish my search of towns along Highway 280, which goes into Alabama, and one of the exits is at just the place where Casey got online in Auburn.

For the next couple of days I focus my efforts in the towns along that corridor, but still nothing. Casey seems to be off the grid. Even the social security Administration doesn't show her getting a job anywhere or applying for a credit card, even under her alias.

I still haven't heard back from all of the police and sheriff's departments. Some of the more rural or smaller towns have small, laid-back departments that probably don't rely that much on technology, so maybe they haven't checked their e-mail. If I don't hear from them in the next couple of days, I'll follow up with phone calls.

I'm getting discouraged when I get a call from the Shady Grove Police Department. "We got your e-mail," a man who introduces himself as Sergeant Baxter tells me. "Sorry we didn't get back to you earlier. We're a little shorthanded and no one saw it until just now."

"Have you got something?" I ask him.

"Yes, as a matter of fact. Grace Newland does live here in Shady Grove."

I almost run off the road, so I pull over into a parking lot. "You're sure?"

"Yes. Dead sure. Picture matches. We arrested her on another charge a couple days ago. She bonded out. If we'd known she was wanted for murder . . ."

"What charge?" I ask, grabbing paper to write all this down.

"Breaking and entering. We could go pick her up, though. We have her address, her car model and tag, her place of employment . . ."

Jackpot! He reads those out to me, and I write them all down. "Tell me about this charge. What did she do?"

Baxter is matter-of-fact. "She was caught breaking in to a basement window of a man named Frank Dotson."

"Did she steal anything?"

"No, she didn't actually get in. Her story was that Dotson was holding a girl there who's been missing for two years."

"What girl?"

"Her name's Laura Daly. Pretty, blonde fourteen-year-old

who was kidnapped after a youth group meeting. People from all over the state turned out to search for her. Never found her."

"No body?"

"Nothing. The case is still open, of course, but we haven't had any solid leads in over a year and a half."

"Until now." I think about this for a moment. For Casey to risk being found, she must really believe the girl is there. She's managed to outwit the police—and me—until now. Something compelling had to happen to make her take that risk.

Or maybe she really is a hardened criminal stealing to get by. "Did you check out her story?" I ask.

"Sure we did. We searched the Dotson house that very night. There wasn't anybody there other than him and his wife. Wife is a known alcoholic. Grace Newland—or Casey, if that's her real name—told us she talked to Laura through a boarded-up window in the basement. She said Laura identified herself. But we're guessing that it was the wife messing with her. Either that, or Casey's delusional."

The Casey I've been learning about is not delusional. Not one of her friends hinted at that, and they would have, because that would have helped explain why she might have committed murder.

"Did you search the basement?"

"Yes. Just like anybody else's basement. Shelves and shelves of junk. Sad thing is that this girl knows the Daly family, and she got them all worked up. Convinced them she'd found Laura, told them she heard a baby crying. So they're thinking not only have they found their missing girl, but that she's got a child. They were devastated when we didn't find her there. They believed Casey. Still do, probably. It's torture for them."

"How does she know them? Did they ever mention that?"

"No, that didn't come up."

I try to imagine who they are to her. Did she come here because she knew them, when she avoided every other connection in her life? Or did she meet them after she got here?

"Can I talk to them? The Dalys?"

"Sure, I don't think it would hurt. They need to understand that they're dealing with a psychopath."

I almost defend her, but I think better of it. He gives me their address. I want to ask for Dotson's address, but I figure I can come up with that on my own.

"So do you want us to bring her back in? We could make an arrest tonight."

I can't believe I'm hesitating. I imagine police cars descending on her apartment complex, drawing the neighbors' attention. Casey coming to the door in her pajamas, being handcuffed and frisked, then paraded out in front of everyone.

I don't want that to happen. I still don't think she's a killer.

"No," I say, knowing I might regret what is surely a lapse in judgment. "I have to be careful about tipping her off. She's really slippery. I want to case her apartment and make sure she's there. Once I'm sure, I'll call you guys to help me make the arrest."

I can tell the sergeant is disappointed. "Okay, we'll stand

down for now. I hope you don't intend to wait. Word flies like wildfire around this town. If one person knows you're asking about her, she'll probably hear about it."

"I won't wait," I say. "I'm on it."

"Do you think she's armed and dangerous?"

I hesitate again. "Was she the other night?"

"No. Not armed at all, except for a crowbar and two screwdrivers. She was adamant that we listen to her about Laura Daly. It was really disappointing to find out she was wrong. We all want to find that girl."

When I click off the phone, I sit in my car for a long moment. I've got her. She's right there, less than an hour away. I'm about to meet the girl who's occupied my thoughts for days.

If I only knew what to do with her.

40

DYLAN

It's dark and there's no light on in Casey's apartment, and a search of the parking lot doesn't turn up her white Kia. Still, I go to the door and knock on it lightly, but I hear nothing inside. Casey must not be home.

Instead of waiting, I head to the Daly house. If they're among her only friends in town, they might know her hangouts. When I knock on the door, an older woman answers. "Hello," she says with a sweet smile. She reminds me of my grandmother.

"Hi," I say, "I'm Dylan Roberts. I'm looking for Sandra Daly."

"She's my daughter," the woman says. "I'm Lucy. Come on in and I'll get her."

I wait just inside the door. Two kids sit in front of the TV. One's doing homework, a binder and textbook in his lap. The other one's got headphones on and is playing a video game. When they look at me I say hi, and they both speak, then return to their activities.

I hear footsteps coming down the stairs, and a younger woman—Sandra, no doubt—approaches me cautiously. Her eyes are red and puffy, and dark circles underlie them.

"Is this about Laura?"

In an instant I'm aware that unannounced visitors to this home may look like messengers of the worst news of her life. "Sort of, but I don't have any new information about her," I say quickly. "Is there somewhere private we can talk?"

She leads me into the kitchen, where she offers me a chair at the table. "What is it, then?" she asks as she sits down. Miss Lucy takes the chair next to her.

I start over, looking from Sandra to her mother. "I'm Dylan Roberts, a private investigator working with the Shreveport, Louisiana, Police Department."

Sandra's hand comes to her chest. "Shreveport? Do you think Laura is there?"

"No, ma'am," I say quickly. "I'm looking for someone else. Grace Newland."

"Grace?" Sandra asks. "What about her?"

"I was hoping you could tell me where she is. I went by her apartment tonight, but she's not home."

Sandra frowns at her mother, then looks back at me. "I don't understand. Why would you come here?"

"The police department told me you're friends. Since it was urgent, they gave me your address. I'm working on a case involving a woman named Casey Cox. We've learned she's here, going by the name of Grace Newland."

Lucy's mouth falls open. "No, you must have the wrong person."

"The Shady Grove police identified her from the pictures. She was arrested the other night."

Lucy's and Sandra's astonished gazes lock. Sandra turns back to me. "Why are you looking for her?" she asks.

I don't want to tell them that she's wanted for murder, so I skirt the issue. "She's wanted for questioning on some things in Shreveport. If you could just tell me where she hangs out, who she might be with . . ."

Lucy gets up suddenly, all traces of her sweetness gone. "I know who you are," she says.

"You do?" I ask.

"Yes. You're that ex-boyfriend of hers. The one she was running from."

I freeze for a moment, my mind searching for a response. "What ex-boyfriend?"

"The one who abused her," Lucy says. "You need to leave."

I don't get up. "No, ma'am, I'm not her boyfriend. I've actually never met her. You can call the police department and verify what I'm saying. I don't know what she told you, but Grace Newland is not who she says she is."

Sandra gets up and grabs the cell phone charging on the counter. She presses just one button—apparently she has the police department on speed dial.

Lucy glares at me like a sentinel as I get to my feet and wait for Sandra to check me out. When her contact confirms that I'm legit, she hangs up and nods to her mother. "They said he's for real. It seems to be true. Grace is wanted for murder."

"But it's a mistake. That girl is not a criminal, and I won't help you find her."

Sandra sighs. "Mama, we have to—"

"No!" The older woman cuts her off. "I know evil. I lived with it for years. You can't tell me she's evil."

"I'm not saying she is," I say. "She may even be innocent. But she's a fugitive from justice. She didn't have a boyfriend. That's just her cover story. But one of her good friends, who happens to be a good friend of mine, too, was murdered brutally, and the police think she did it. She's been in hiding ever since."

Lucy's face pales, and I worry she might faint. Sandra goes to her and puts her arms around her.

"She hasn't asked for anything from us," Lucy says, "and she wouldn't take what we wanted to give her."

Sandra's hands move to her mouth. "We offered her a place

to live in the apartment over the garage, but she refused." She notices the kids standing in the kitchen doorway now. "Boys, go upstairs."

"But I want to hear," the older one says.

"Upstairs, now!" Sandra says sharply, and they disappear. I hear footsteps go partway up. I know they're listening at the top.

"Mrs. Daly, how did you meet her?" I ask.

Sandra looks at her mother, then Lucy speaks up. Her voice is low, weak. "I met her on the bus coming from home."

"Home?" I ask. "Where was that?"

"Oklahoma."

Of course. She was probably Casey's seatmate for hours and hours, and Casey struck up a friendship with the woman and decided to go where she went. "So how long has she been here?"

"Three weeks . . . maybe a month," Lucy says. "I can't believe she would've done the things you're saying. Not this girl. She couldn't. She wouldn't hurt a flea."

Sandra sits back down and starts to cry. "We believed that she talked to Laura. We still want to believe her, unless you're telling us that she's crazy, that she's some kind of maniac."

"She's not," Lucy insists. "I'm telling you, she's not. I've been around liars my whole life. She's not like them."

"She has lied to you," I say softly. "I can't guarantee that she's a murderer. I've just been hired to bring her back. If she's innocent, I'm sure justice will be served. But you've got to tell me where she is."

"Is she dangerous?" Sandra asks, looking toward the stairs.

"I don't think she is, but I can't guarantee it."

"Is she wanted for murder or not?" she asks.

"She is," I say, knowing I sound insane myself, "and if you don't tell me what you know about her, she might get away."

Sandra bursts into tears. "I wanted to believe her," she says. "I wanted to think that she really talked to Laura, even though the police didn't find her there."

"She may have been telling the truth," I say.

"But according to you she's a liar and a murderer!"

Her hope is vaporizing right before my eyes, but I don't dare give her false hope.

"We were so close," Lucy says. "We thought we were going to find her. We were going to get her back."

"All I know," I say, "is that I've been hired to find Casey Cox and bring her home, and I have to do that with or without you. But if you hide her whereabouts, you could become an accessory to murder."

Sandra stands back up. "Are you kidding me?"

These people have been tormented enough, so I don't repeat it. "One last time. Do you have any idea where she could be?"

"No!" Lucy says. "She goes to work and comes home, and that's about it up until a few days ago. She was watching the Dotson house a lot. We didn't know it until she broke in and got arrested, but then she told us everything."

Sandra sinks back into her chair. Her voice is monotone. "Mama, none of it was real. Just accept it now."

"No," Lucy says. "I won't accept it. Until we find Laura's body, she *is* alive. She's *somewhere!*"

Sandra rubs her fingers down her face, then looks up at me. "We're telling the truth. If Grace isn't home, we don't know where she is."

"Is she dating anybody? Does she have any other friends? Her coworkers?"

"She's actually a very friendly person," Lucy says, "just a ray of sunshine, or so it seemed. I adore her. She makes friends easily. I just don't know any of them."

It seems everyone who knows Casey personally adores her. When I leave that devastated family, I drive back to Casey's apartment. Her car still isn't there.

It's just a matter of time. She has to come home eventually.

41

CASEY

It's been a long day at work, and Laura Daly's plight has kept me constantly distracted. When I get off, I go straight to the Dotsons' street and try to figure out a way to prove Laura's been there.

When my phone rings, I see that it's Miss Lucy. I answer quickly.

"Grace, thank heaven!" she says.

Miss Lucy sounds as if she's been crying, and she speaks in a low voice, as though she doesn't want to be overheard. "Miss Lucy? Is everything all right?"

"Grace, there was someone here asking about you just now."

My breath catches. I pull my car out of the parking lot, alert now to anyone who might be following. "What? Who?"

"A man who told us that Grace is not your real name." Her tone is flat, resigned.

I let out a miserable sigh. "Dylan Roberts?"

She's silent for a moment, then she says, "Is it true, the things he said?"

I'm sunk. It's over. I can't go home now. "I don't know what he said," I tell her. "But it's true that I'm hiding from the police."

Lucy's gasp is audible. "I couldn't believe it! You *killed* somebody?"

"No, I didn't!" I say. "Miss Lucy, you know I'm not the kind of person who could hurt anyone."

"But you're lying about who you are, where you came from. Tell me the truth. Were you lying about Laura too?"

"No, absolutely not! Miss Lucy, I heard her. I talked to her. That's true. Please believe me."

"How can I? Sandra's devastated. She's lost all hope."

I lean my head back on the seat and close my eyes. "Miss Lucy, my father was murdered when I was twelve, by dirty cops. They made it look like a suicide. It's haunted me for years, and my friend who was a reporter started investigating it and got too close to the truth. He wound up murdered too. I found his body, so my DNA is everywhere."

Miss Lucy's silent for a moment, taking it in. Her voice is

more empathetic when she speaks again. "Then go back and tell them that. Hiding makes you look guilty. Take it from me, honey. There will be people who believe you."

"Not if they kill me first. You don't understand this kind of evil."

"Honey, I've dealt with police. Most of them are honest. But if some are trying to kill you . . ." Her voice trails off. When she speaks again, her words are raspy. "I don't know what to tell you, other than . . . I believe you."

I press my fist against my forehead. "Miss Lucy, I want you to know that you've meant a lot to me. You've saved my life, given me a reason to live. I have lied to you, and you didn't deserve that."

Miss Lucy is weeping now. She steadies her voice and says, "Grace . . . Casey . . . whatever your name is . . . God can forgive you. He moved heaven and earth to make it possible to wipe your slate clean. He may not clear up all the charges against you, but he can heal your heart and help you through this. If you've ever listened to anything I've said, listen to that."

"I am listening," I say, my face twisted. "Thank you, Miss Lucy."

I cut my connection to her and press the phone to my heart. Suddenly I miss my mom with an ache that cuts through my bones.

I start my car, crying and wondering if I should just turn around and drive out of town.

But what about Laura? I know Dotson has her. No one believes me.

I can't stand the thought of Sandra weeping through the night, crushed that her last hope for Laura rested on the word of a liar. I have to fix it. I have to see this through. For Sandra and for Laura . . . but mostly for Miss Lucy, who still believes in me.

It starts to drizzle, and I look up to the heavens through my rain-streaked windshield. "God, if she's right . . . if you're there . . . if you care at all, then give me the courage to do what's right."

What a farce—praying to God to help you break a law! What am I thinking? But doesn't God love Laura? Doesn't he want her to be set free? Isn't saving a kidnapped girl's life the *right* thing?

I swallow my tears. "If you could just give me courage," I plead again. My voice breaks off, and I hope this God of Miss Lucy's can see through the mess of my heart and cut right to the motives. I want to save Laura, even if it means I can no longer save myself.

I don't go home. I never can again. Everything in my apartment will have to be left behind. What little I've been carrying in my car will have to get me through.

42

CASEY

Not only am I a fugitive, I'm premeditating breaking and entering again. That makes me a criminal even if I've never killed anyone.

At Home Depot, I get out in the drizzling rain and check the trunk of my car. There's a jack in a compartment next to the spare tire, along with a pry bar. I shove the bar into my backpack, since the police kept my crowbar. I try to think it through. There's a padlock on the outside cellar door. I need bolt cutters.

I pull my hair up in a ponytail and put on my Braves baseball cap to shelter my face from cameras, then I hurry in and grab the biggest bolt cutters I can find, along with a flashlight, and check out.

Then I drive to the Dotsons' house again. Their car isn't there, so I drive by the bar to see if Frank and Arelle are there. They are, so I hurry back. I have to get into that house. It's now or never. I park my car up the street, slip on my backpack, and walk to their house, but this time I avoid the side of the house where the neighbor called the police. I go around the opposite side, next to a big fence enclosing the other neighbor's yard. It's raining harder now, soaking my shirt and jeans.

In the backyard, I position the bolt cutter blades over the padlock on the cellar door and squeeze. I'm not strong enough to snap it cleanly, but I work at it and finally cut through the metal. I pull the padlock off and pull on the door handles—the doors don't budge. They must be locked from inside too. Frank Dotson was thorough.

I can't give up, so I go back to the side of the house. There's a window that must be a bedroom, maybe the master. I drop my backpack on the dirt and pull out a T-shirt. I hold it against the glass to muffle the sound, then tap it with the pry bar. The glass cracks nicely. I wrap the T-shirt around my hand, then knock away enough of the glass that I can reach in and unlock the sash. The glass shards don't make much noise as they fall, so I assume there's carpet below.

I raise the sash, then look into the dark room. I dust the glass off the pane, lift myself up, and climb into what looks like a guest room. I close the window and pull the curtains shut.

I use my flashlight to look around the room. There's a twin bed in a corner. The place is dusty and has a vinegar-like smell. I leave that room and go up the hall to the den off the kitchen. The furniture is old, the upholstery split and oozing batting. I go into the kitchen and see the sidebar behind the table, the one in the picture that showed Laura Daly's article. It's gone now. I'm sure Dotson discarded it before the police searched, just as he might have somehow done with Laura.

I look around for the basement door. There it is, right next to the refrigerator. I hurry across the room, throw it open, and shine my beam into deeper darkness. I go down the stairs carefully. Since I know the windows are boarded, I turn on the light.

At the bottom, I look across the room and see the cellar doors at the top of another set of concrete steps. As I thought, it's padlocked from inside. Shelves line the walls. There's no sign of Laura.

Still, I call out. "Laura? Laura? Are you here?"

There's only silence.

Since the basement light is dim, I shine the flashlight around the tops of the walls, trying to get my bearings. Where was the window I tried to get through the other night? It wasn't the window near the corner of the house—I can see that one, and it's boarded up too, but I know it's not the one. There was another one. I don't see it. Maybe they've moved the shelves in front of it and stacked them with things to camouflage it. I step in that direction and move a toolbox, an old boat motor, a box with a tangle of cables, a wadded tarp. There's nothing but cinderblock wall behind the shelves.

No wonder the police gave up. There's really nothing to see here.

Exhausted, I sit on the stairs, wondering if I've imagined the whole thing. Am I losing it? Did I really talk to Laura Daly? Did I really hear a baby?

Tears push to my eyes. Is it possible that I imagined it all? Am I so desperate to solve someone else's problems, since I can't solve my own, that my brain would manufacture something this bizarre?

No. I'm *not* crazy. I'm not an alarmist. I'm not a drama queen. Anyone who knows me knows that. I heard what I heard.

I try again, louder. "Laura? Laura, please, if you're here, say something! I don't know where to look."

Nothing.

One more time, I shine my flashlight around the walls, desperate for any sign that Laura was here. No footprints in the dust on the floor, no diaper pail, no baby supplies.

But that missing window plagues me. Where could it be?

Again, I shine the light slowly along the top of each wall. There are two boarded-up windows in here, and only two. I know I counted three windows outside. I try to orient myself. The one I heard Laura through wouldn't be on this side of the house.

I can't accomplish anything here. I go back up, closing the basement door behind me. I shine my light through the house, checking every room and every closet for any sign of Laura, or of any place Dotson might have taken her. There's nothing. No baby equipment. No diapers in the trash. No careless notes with an address of some secret hiding place.

What if he's already killed and disposed of them?

Sick at the thought, I realize it's time to leave. I open the side door that opens into the carport, but before I can step out, headlights sweep across the carport's back wall and grow larger as a car pulls up the driveway. I jump back inside, close the door. I turn and look around, panicked. I can't go out the front door, and I don't see a back one. I hurry back through the house to the room I broke in to. I start to open the damp curtains to climb back through, but then I hear their voices.

I freeze, listening. Maybe they'll talk about Laura. Maybe they'll mention where she is.

Instead of escaping, I hide behind that room's door and strain to hear.

They're both clearly inebriated. Their words are slurred.

"Need to go down and check on her," he says.

"Don hurt her again," the woman says, her words running together. "Just leave her be for tonight. I don't wanna take care of the baby. Come to bed."

My heart jolts. They're talking about Laura! She's in the house. *Down* must mean that she's in the basement. But where? A secret room? There weren't any doors.

Determined to find her, I resolve to stay. I will find her. I'll spend the night here if I have to.

43

CASEY

I try to slow my breathing as I stand in the dark behind the door in the guest room. Dotson and his wife turn on the TV and make something to eat. I wait, afraid to move, worried they'll see my wet footprints or hear the rain dripping through the broken window. But they apparently haven't noticed either. Finally, I hear Dotson's phlegmy snoring on the couch. What if he sleeps there all night, and I'm stuck here? I should leave now, but then I'd have to leave Laura again. This time when I leave, I can never come back.

Finally, Arelle wakes him up. "Come to bed," she says again in her raspy, smoky voice. "Come on, get up."

"Have to check on them," he mutters as he walks back to the bedroom next door to where I stand. The floor squeaks with every step.

"Do it later," she says. "Leave 'em alone for tonight."

I listen as they grow quiet, and I imagine they've gotten into bed. After a while, I hear him snoring again.

I move out from around the door. I tiptoe up the hall into the den, see the food bowls out on the table, soggy cereal congealing in milk. I get to the basement door, pull it open.

It squeaks loudly. Why hadn't I noticed that before? I hear movement from the bedroom, so I hurry away from the door, across the room. The floor squeaks in the hall. I dive under the table, the yellowed tablecloth hiding me.

"Do you want to die?" I jump as Frank Dotson's voice bellows. He knows I'm here! I crouch under the table, holding my breath as he stomps through to the kitchen. The light comes on, flooding the room and casting long shadows that seem to point to me. He's going to kill me and no one will know. Murder is my destiny. It's going to happen to me one way or another.

But then he curses and throws open the basement door. "What are you doing?" he yells down.

He's not talking to me. I hear him thump down the stairs, curses flying. I don't hear anything from Laura, but now I'm sure she's here. I tiptoe across the floor again, knowing it will creak beneath my feet, but maybe he'll think it's Arelle. If Laura's there, I need to know how to get to her. I peer through the basement door and see him going to a shelf, shoving it out of the way. Nothing but cinderblocks there, but then I see a rectangle opening up. It's an optical illusion, wood painted to look like cement blocks. I should have seen it! I realize it's the old coal chute. Of course! It must be closed in at the top, and that's where that broken patio is.

"You're a slow learner!" he bellows in. What are you doing to the ceiling? It woke me up!"

A baby's cry rises in startled terror, and my gut hitches.

"I didn't do anything!" I hear a girl saying in a dry, brittle voice. Laura! "We were sleeping. You woke her up! Please. We didn't do anything. You said yourself you can't hear us through all the padding. I can't even reach the ceiling. I don't have anything to stand on."

A shiver goes through me. If he's angry or drunk enough, my carelessness—the very sound of my footsteps—might get her killed. I shrink back into the kitchen. The storm outside gets angrier, and rain pounds against the roof, the windows. Thunder cracks as if God himself is reacting to this evil. Somehow, that gives me courage. I head back up the hall to the guest room, praying that if Dotson hears my steps he'll think it's his wife. I wait behind the door, shaking.

I think of escaping through the window while I still can, going straight back to the police, turning myself in but demanding that they search again for the coal chute where Laura is hidden. But their main focus will be the murderer hiding out in Shady Grove, rather than the rescue of the missing girl. They won't listen to me. Why should they?

My courage wanes, and paralysis freezes me. No, I can't freeze. I have to act.

My brave girl.

Tears come to my eyes again, and I wipe them on my sleeve. No time to cry. I have to move.

I hear him striking her, things crashing, her abbreviated yelps. I wait as the door to the coal chute crashes shut—silencing the baby's cries completely—as Dotson comes up from the basement, slams the door, and pounds his way back to bed.

I wait longer this time, certain that he's snoring rhythmically before I venture out. The storm is loud now, a symphony of percussion against the house, lightning flashing and thunder cracking quick behind it. Is that answered prayer, meant to disguise my steps? Can I assume God is really helping me? Maybe Miss Lucy is praying too.

Tears wet my face again, and I wipe them away, force myself to draw in a cleansing breath. I take huge steps to make fewer creaks, and I make it to the basement door. I don't open it wide, because I can't risk another squeak. I slip through the gap, turn on the light, and quietly steal down the stairs.

He's pushed the shelf unit back to the wall, but I know which one it is. I move it as quietly as I can, an inch at a time, constantly checking the top of the stairs. I'm running on pure adrenaline now, desperate to get to that little door.

Finally, I make enough room behind the shelves to open the door. I twist the deadbolt up and pull the camouflaged door open.

The room is tiny, damp and cold, and smells of diapers. It's dark and only a few feet wide. There's an extension cord going under the door, lighting a small yellow lamp. I should have noticed that cord before. The baby is sleeping on a mattress on the floor, wearing a dingy pink onesie. Laura's in a fetal position on the concrete next to the mattress. She looks dead.

"Laura?" I whisper loudly.

She startles awake, sucks in a breath, and looks at me. "Who are you?"

Her eye is black and bloody, her nose looks broken. She has a busted lower lip, and when she sits up, I can see that her knee is purple and swollen. He has beaten her up because of me.

I hold out a shaky hand to quiet her. "I'm Grace. I've come to get you out of here."

Her lower lip trembles. "Are . . . are they here?"

"Yes. They're sleeping. The storm is loud. We have to hurry, though. We can go out the cellar door. I broke the lock on the outside . . . and I have bolt cutters for the inside lock."

She grabs up her sleeping baby. She looks like she's Emma's age. The child keeps sleeping as Laura clutches her to her chest.

"I can't walk . . . my knee . . ."

"Do the best you can," I say, going in and putting her arm around my shoulders. "I'll help you. Come on. They seem drunk and they're sleeping hard."

She hobbles out with me, and I feel her ribs under my fingertips. She's skeletal, as if every ounce of fat has wasted out of her. I wonder how often he feeds her. She shifts the baby to the side with the strong leg, and I get under her other arm and help her walk. Each step makes her grind her teeth in pain. We get to the concrete steps leading up to the cellar hatch. I go up first. There's a two-by-four bolted across the double-bulkhead door. One end of the two-by-four is fastened with an old hinge, and on the other, there's another lock with a padlock slipped through. I slip off my backpack and take out my bolt cutters.

"I've got this," I tell Laura, who has dragged herself up three of the dozen or so stairs and waits with her baby just below me.

I try with all my might to cut the padlock, but at this angle, reaching above my head, I'm not strong enough. I can hear the rain pounding through the wood, and some of it leaks through, wetting the concrete stairs. We're so close . . .

Then the baby starts to cry.

44

DYLAN

I sit in Casey's apartment parking lot for another hour, watching through my wet windshield for her white Kia to pull in, but it never does. Where could she be? Lucy and Sandra said she doesn't have hangouts, that she's basically been obsessed with finding Laura.

Maybe she's watching the Dotson house again. It's worth a look. I'm pulling out of the parking lot when my phone rings. I glance at it, see Keegan's name.

I click it on. "Hello?"

He sounds excited. "Why didn't you call me, Dylan? I heard from the Shady Grove, Georgia, PD that you found Casey Cox."

My chest tightens. "I haven't found her. They say she's here, but I don't have eyes on her yet."

"But you have her alias and address and car model, right? Put out a BOLO and let the force locate her car."

"I'm trying to keep from tipping her off," I say as I drive. "For all I know, she's listening to the scanner. I'm close. Just let me finish doing my job."

"Listen, I'm getting on a plane right now."

I pull off the road into a Zaxby's parking lot to keep from wrecking. "To come here?"

"Yeah. Buddy of mine has a Cessna. I'll be there in a few hours and take it over."

My stomach tightens. "Look, that might be premature. I don't know if she's even still here. Besides, the weather's horrible. I don't know if you can land here."

"My buddy's a pro. He can handle it."

I clear my throat and try again. "She could have left town. I've been waiting at her apartment for hours and she hasn't come home. I'd hate for you to come all the way here, risking this weather, if it's just a dead end."

Keegan is quiet for a minute. "Dylan, you're scaring me, man. First I hear about this from the Shady Grove department instead of you, now you're downplaying this huge development? You know this find makes you a shoo-in for a spot on the force, right? I will personally recommend you for the Major Crimes Unit. We have a detective retiring next month. But if you drop the ball on this—"

"Drop the ball? I'm not dropping the ball. I'm looking for her as we speak. All I'm saying is, hold off coming here until I have her in custody. I'll call the local cops when I have eyes on her, and they'll make the arrest and hold her until you come."

"No can do. I'm too pumped about this, my man. Besides, I love night flying. It's a blast. I'm coming. Rollins doesn't like to fly, so he's driving once I tell him we have her. Man's a wimp." His laugh cuts through my blood.

I know from Brent's files that the plane belongs to Keegan. He's flying himself, and when he gets here and takes over, I'll have no control. I doubt seriously he would put Casey on that plane and fly her back alone. Does he plan to take her back at all?

The job prospect sounds real. I want it so badly, my heart thuds at the thought. But if Keegan "takes over" with Casey, she might wind up dead before she's extradited.

He's clicked off the call, so I pull back out into the trickle of traffic and head to the Dotsons' street. My thoughts race. What if I find her and take her in, then get Brent's files to key people in the department—the chief seems untarnished, and there are bound to be others. I could give it to several cops at the same time.

I turn onto Dotson's street, drive by his house. The lights

are off, a car in the carport. I've driven past a few more houses when I see her car—a white Kia—parked on the curb.

She isn't in it. Where has she gone?

A chill shivers down my spine.

Casey may be in that house.

45

CASEY

At the sound of the baby crying, I spin back toward Laura, palm down, as if that will silence the baby.

Laura tries to muffle the baby's face against her chest. "Hurry!" she whispers.

I can't make the heavy bolt cutters work. Instead, I try to push the bolt up, hoping the wood is rotten or that the hinge or lock is loose, but nothing budges.

I look back toward the stairs up into the house. If they're still sleeping, if the noise of the storm keeps masking our sounds, maybe we could go through the kitchen. No, that would never work with the baby crying. This is our only way. I try the bolt again.

The door from the kitchen suddenly flies open, and Laura screams. Dotson's silhouette at the top of the stairs is stark in the kitchen light. He yells, then flies down the stairs, crosses the basement in three steps to the concrete steps we're scaling, grabs Laura and backhands her, knocking her off her feet. I grab the baby out of her arms as she falls. It screams two octaves higher. Laura cries out in pain as she hits the cement floor, her head thudding. Clutching the writhing child with one arm, I heft up the bolt cutters and swing them at Dotson as he comes after me. His eyes are bloodshot and murderous, and he gropes for the child. I swing again, but my movement is awkward, and he snatches the tool away. How will I get us out now? I climb back to the double doors over my head and bang with all my might, screaming for help.

I should have called the police. They *might* have come, if only to apprehend me.

The baby is terrorized, leaning her weight toward her mom as Laura gets up and lunges at Dotson, struggling to block the bolt cutters with her skinny arms.

I bang harder with one hand on the doors over me, feel them give slightly. Rain seeps in through the edges. If the wood is rotten, maybe it will splinter open with enough force, in spite of the lock.

Dotson grabs my foot, and I cushion the baby's head as I hit one step, then get dragged to the next.

I flip to a sitting position, holding the baby too tight. Her screams pierce my ears.

I yell for help, hoping the neighbor will hear me or Laura. I get back up as Dotson lunges up toward me. I kick and thrash at him, desperate not to drop the baby. I get one good kick into his jaw, then aim lower. I hit home, and he doubles over, grunting. I scramble to my feet, grab the bolt cutters back.

"Run!" Laura screams. "Take her and get out!"

Even if I could open the door, I can't leave Laura there. Dotson rises again, his teeth bared as he comes at me. I kick at him, then lift up and bang again on the doors with the bolt cutters. I lose my footing and slip down one step, but I cushion the baby. My shin is bruised and bloody, but I swing the tool at him again.

Below us, Laura grabs a steel pipe lying against the wall. She comes back and swings at him, hitting his knee and knocking his foot out from under him. He falls and catches himself a few steps down.

I pray to God that the neighbor will hear our screams, that she'll call the police again. But the storm is too loud. What helped me moments earlier is now my greatest obstacle.

Then I see Arelle staggering down the basement stairs. "Stop it!" she yells.

"Help me!" Dotson cries. "Arelle, get the gun!"

She freezes for a moment as Laura swings again, this time hitting the back of Dotson's skull. Laura backs up as he falls, his legs going limp as he tumbles to the concrete floor.

Arelle runs back up the stairs, and I reach toward Laura with the bolt cutters. She grabs them and I pull her up until she's just below me.

"Stop!"

Arelle stands at the top of the stairs with a shotgun. "Stop!" she shouts again.

Dotson lifts himself to all fours, gets his feet under him.

I get up the steps to the hatch, but I can't hold the baby and work the bolt cutter, so I bang on it with the tool again, and more rain pours in. I scream louder for help, but Arelle will kill us all before I get it open. I hear her chamber a round, sense her aiming.

Suddenly there's a crash above my head, and the doors fly open. Rain pours in, soaking my face. A man stands there, silhouetted by a streetlight.

"Casey!" he says. "Take my hand."

I don't know who he is, but I thrust the baby at him and turn for Laura. She's still fighting Dotson as Arelle takes aim. I leap down and hurl myself onto Dotson's back. "Go!" I yell, and Laura limps up the first three stairs, gritting her teeth. She pulls herself up faster than I thought she could.

Dotson wrestles me off his back, pivots, and swings. His fist crashes across my jaw and knocks me to the floor. Falling, I get a glimpse of Laura escaping out into the night. I'm disoriented, dizzy, as I grapple to get to my feet.

Then I see our rescuer coming in from outside, his eyes pale and his hair wet. As Dotson braces to deliver the knockout punch, the man delivers it instead. Dotson is knocked back to the floor, several feet from me.

As I try to get up, the gun goes off, its blast burning into my soul.

46

DYLAN

The moment the battered girl emerged from the basement into the rain, she lunged for her baby. I handed her over, gave the girl a quick look to make sure she didn't have life-threatening injuries, then gave her my car keys, pointed to my car, and told her to wait there. I'd already called the police and reported screams from the house, before I got the cellar door open. Now I hear sirens approaching in the distance.

As Casey screams, rage drives me back toward the cellar doors. Dotson is going to kill her. I see him strike her, drawing blood. I fly down the steps, leap toward him, and knock him flat on his face. Casey writhes on the floor. Dotson wrestles and tries to get up.

My heart lurches as the gun fires. *Casey!*

But it's not Casey who drops. It's Dotson. I look up at his wife, bracing for her to correct her mistake, but she doesn't. She tosses the gun to the bottom of the stairs—it hits with a clatter. Then she sits down.

I grab the gun and check Dotson. He has a bullet through his head, and he has no pulse. Giving the wife a cautious look, I take Casey's hand, help her up the steps, out into the rain. "Are you all right?" I ask when we're clear of that place.

"Where're Laura and the baby?" she asks.

"In my car. I think they're both all right."

Lightning illuminates the sky for a second, and our eyes lock. I see how blue hers are. I didn't realize they were that blue. Rain drizzles into them, washing the blood from her swelling jaw.

"You're him, aren't you?" she asks. "Dylan Roberts."

"Yes." The sirens grow louder. "They're coming," I say.

She doesn't run away, doesn't look afraid. Then my phone rings. I take it off my belt clip and glance at the caller.

"Keegan," she says.

Now I see the fear as she stares up at me, her pale skin glistening in the next lightning flash. I put the phone back on its clip. "He's flying here tonight to take over my case."

She takes that in, but instead of speaking, she simply turns and walks away, across the muddy grass to the street, toward her Kia that waits a few houses down.

I could grab her, cuff her, easily restrain her.

But I let her go.

Blue lights come from the opposite end of the street, their haze casting an aura over my car where Laura and her baby wait. I glance back toward Casey. Her Kia pulls out into the street and disappears around the corner.

As the first responders get out of their cruisers, I meet them in the street and show them where I have Laura Daly and her baby, and tell them Frank Dotson is dead in the basement. I give them the shotgun and tell them his wife is still in there alive.

They find her wailing on the basement floor next to his body. I may never know if she shot him by mistake in all the confusion or if she meant to kill him.

I go to the police station with Laura and her child and wait with her while her mother is called. Laura makes sure the police know that some girl named Grace is the hero who rescued her. They know it's Casey Cox, and the search for her begins. I tell them what I saw, leaving out the part about my letting her walk away. I let them believe she got away during the chaos.

Miss Lucy and Sandra show up at the station in minutes, and the reunion brings the room to tears. They embrace Laura, almost crushing her in their joy, then kiss the baby as if they've always known her. I know they'll heal Laura's outer wounds. But some wounds can't be seen. I pray that she'll get the help she needs.

When Keegan arrives a couple of hours later, I sit through

a debriefing, telling him every detail of what happened up to Casey getting away. While he curses and rails about my incompetence, I stare at him, wondering how I will find enough evidence to bring him to justice for his crimes. I won't let them be covered up. When they come out, they will come out in a way that is impossible for him to escape. He will pay for his sins.

And I'll make sure he never gets his hands on Casey Cox.

47

CASEY

'm soaking wet and shaking. I'm an hour out of town before I can take in a normal breath. They're not following me. I stop and go into a truck stop, buy a T-shirt and some sweatpants, then change into dry clothes. I buy another prepaid phone. Back in my car, I use the old one and punch in the number I've been longing to call.

It rings four times.

I watch the dark road through the blur of tears.

"Hello?"

"Mom?"

My mother's breath hitches. "Casey, is that you? Thank God, you're alive!"

"Yes," I say as tears pull at my face. "Mom, I miss you."

"I miss you too, honey. Where are you?"

"That doesn't matter," I say. "I just wanted you to know it's gonna be okay."

"Casey, let me come get you."

If only. "No, Mom. I hope you know I didn't do what they're saying."

"Honey, I know that!" I hear her whisper as she repeats her words.

"I know, but . . . I don't want you to have any doubts."

"How could I doubt you?"

I squeeze my eyes shut, and my face stretches across my grief. "Be careful, Mom."

"They're looking for you. That Dylan guy. He's been here asking all about you."

"I know. It's okay." Silence as I hear her sniffs. "Mom? Are you taking your medication?"

"Yes," she says. "I just . . . I don't want you to be caught. Honey, what if you just came back and turned yourself in, and we could get you a lawyer and work it all out?"

I know I'd never survive until a trial could clear me. Keegan would see to that. But I'm glad my mother said that, in case they're listening. "Can't do that, Mom. But I'll be okay. I'll try to call you again soon."

"Casey, promise me you'll come home if things get too dangerous. *Promise me!*"

"Mom, I'm doing my best." I hang on the line for a moment, absorbing comfort from her presence. "Mom, do you pray?"

She lets out a breath into the phone. "I do now." Her voice is broken, high-pitched. "I pray for you constantly."

"Those prayers are being answered," I say. "There is a God, and he listens." I hear her whisper the words back to me.

I don't want to hang up, but they're probably tracing my call, maybe even dispatching police to whatever town I'm in, rushing to pick me up. "I won't be able to call again for a while, but I love you, Mom. I have to go now."

"I love you too, sweetheart."

I click the phone off, roll down my window, and toss it out into a field.

By morning I can be in North Carolina or Virginia or Tennessee. I can buy another new phone and start over. Trade my car. Until then, the tag I took off a car in the Kroger parking lot will have to do.

Grace Newland is really dead now. I'll find another identity, another job, another place in this world where I can try to belong. I'll keep my head low until I have the courage to lift it.

As I drive north, I comfort myself with the fact that Frank Dotson didn't win. This time, evil was conquered.

Keegan and his cohorts didn't win either.

Freedom will have to console me for now.

A NOTE FROM THE AUTHOR

As I've finished the last few steps of getting this book ready for publication, things have happened that have changed the United States drastically. The news about Christians being run out of business for their religious beliefs and baby parts being sold off after abortions, among other things, not only trouble me deeply but turn my stomach. It's difficult to sleep when these things run through our minds.

In the United States, Christians don't face the persecution that our brothers and sisters in other parts of the world face. Some of them are being beheaded because they won't renounce their faith, and schoolgirls are being kidnapped and murdered if they won't renounce, and even if they do, they're married off to evil men. In America, we do still have freedom, yet many of us suffer personal issues—family issues, wayward children, health problems—things that drain the life out of us and make us *feel* persecuted. Part of that is due to the fallen world we live in (Christians are not immune), and part is due to spiritual attacks against us. "For our struggle is not against flesh and blood, but against the rulers, against the powers, against the world forces of this darkness, against the spiritual forces of wickedness in the heavenly places" (Ephesians 6:12).

With all that weighing heavily on me, my husband and I took a cruise to Alaska. I've seen some beautiful places, but I've never seen anything as beautiful as the mountain peaks in Juneau, Alaska, or the constantly moving and changing glaciers in Glacier Bay. We took a helicopter ride over those mountains on a rare sunny day, and every time we crested a mountain peak, I gasped audibly at the stunning majesty of what I saw. Then we landed on the Mendenhall Glacier, suited up and booted up, and walked around on that blue ice for an hour.

As I beheld the creativity of our Creator, I wondered how anyone can see such natural art and not understand the existence and power of God. Seriously, you think all this came from some cosmic explosion? Or evolution? The idea that there are so many beautiful and magnificent things working and fitting together in such a precise and elegant way flies in the face of Darwin's theories. There is a God, and he is the most powerful force in the universe. He created those beautiful mountains and glaciers, untouched by human hands, and he created you and me. And though he controls the movement of glaciers and the forest fires that allow new growth and the earthquakes that push mountains up from the ground so that the landscape is ever-changing, he loves us enough to personally guide us if we'll let him, enough to make a way for us to be with him in his home forever. As beautiful as our planet is now, it's going to be even more glorious when he creates a new heaven and a new earth (see Revelation 21 and 22). He has told us in the Bible how this world is going to end, and as frightening—and familiar—as it is, we know that the end times are only the beginning of the great things God has planned for his people.

I admit I was a little depressed when I came back home after such an experience. Bad news is still being reported, and personal issues loom. But as discouragement began to sink back in, I read a prophecy about Jesus from Isaiah 42.

> Behold, My Servant, whom I uphold;
> My chosen one in whom My soul delights.
> I have put My Spirit upon Him;
> He will bring forth justice to the nations.
> He will not cry out or raise His voice,
> Nor make His voice heard in the street.
> A bruised reed He will not break
> And a dimly burning wick He will not extinguish;
> He will faithfully bring forth justice.
> He will not be disheartened or crushed
> Until He has established justice in the earth.
> (vv. 1–4)

Knowing that Jesus will not be disheartened or crushed, that he won't feel the need to shout in the streets or rail against anything, that he will bring forth justice in the twinkle of an eye, encourages me. Things look grim, but God is still in control. Sometimes terrible things happen in our culture. Logic seems upside down, and the masses march to the drumbeat of political correctness. Our job is to stand up for our beliefs, cling to them no matter what, and wait for our redemption. Jesus will not let us down.

I hope this encourages you today.

DISCUSSION QUESTIONS

1. Discuss Casey's options after finding Brent dead. How do you feel about her running?
2. Would you rather be in prison for something you didn't do or hide out alone for the rest of your life? What would starting over with a new identity in a new place—alone—be like for you?
3. How has Casey's faith (or lack thereof) impacted her choices? Would she have seen things differently if she'd believed in God?
4. How did Casey's view of God change during this book?
5. How has Brent's PTSD impacted his search for Casey?
6. Why would Casey feel comfortable being a hero for Laura, but not for herself?
7. Do you think Casey is brave or cowardly? Why?

8. How does Dylan's faith impact his choices? Did he make the right choice at the end?
9. Casey thinks she's cowardly. Do you agree with her?
10. There are two more books coming in this trilogy. Discuss what you would like to see happen.

ACKNOWLEDGMENTS

Years ago a friend had a dream. In the dream, my husband, Ken, was standing on the ground, and I was flying around in the sky. He had the distinct impression that my husband was somehow anchoring me while I soared. Years have passed since that dream, and in so many ways, it has been fulfilled. Without Ken tethering me, I probably would have sped off like a deflating balloon and crashed, unnoticed. He is always steadfast in my life, always inspires me, always makes me laugh, always encourages me to keep flying, and always points me to the One who is the true anchor for both of us. Ken often takes flight himself to do the things he's been called to do, but he never lets go of me. He's one of the greatest gifts God has given me.

I also want to take a moment to thank some crucial people in my publishing process, because they're the behind-the-scenes heroes who make sure my books are ready for my readers. I don't know if most people understand how much work goes into my books. Though writing is a labor of love, it's something that gets harder with each new story. Maybe it's because I don't want to let my readers down and I'm so focused on offering a fresh new read.

Whatever the reason, I'm so grateful for the editors who work tirelessly to help me take my books to the next level. They point out what changes need to be made, and I take those suggestions and rewrite so many times that I almost have the book memorized by the time it's on the shelves. I'm especially grateful to Dave Lambert, who's edited almost all of my books for the last twenty years. I'm also very thankful for Amanda Bostic, Ellen Tarver, and Jodi Hughes, all of whom worked on *If I Run*. Without these amazing people, I would be a very insecure writer.

Beyond editorial, I'm grateful for Daisy Hutton, Fiction Publisher of HarperCollins Christian Publishing. She has been a joy to work with and a bright spot in my life. I'm also grateful for Katie Bond, the amazing marketing director who creatively finds ways to help readers discover my books. I'm thankful to Sue Brower, who started out as my marketing director twenty years ago, then was one of my editors, then became my agent. Kristen Ingebretson, who creates my cover designs, is also crucial to the process. So many others are instrumental in the publishing and marketing of my books.

The thought of all the details they handle so seamlessly just overwhelms me. I thank all of them.

And to my loyal readers, thank you for hanging in there with me all these years. Without your word of mouth and your enthusiasm for my books, I wouldn't be able to continue doing what I love.

Terri Blackstock loves to hear from readers, receiving your letters and visiting via social media and her newsletter. Connect with her at www.TerriBlackstock.com or on Facebook at https://www.facebook.com/tblackstock.

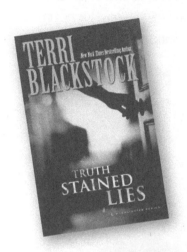
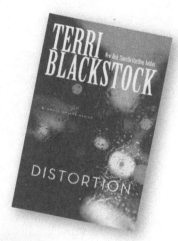
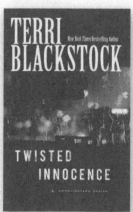

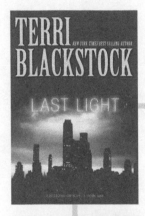
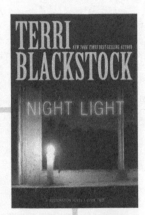
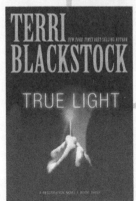
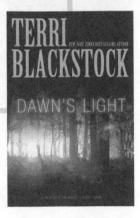

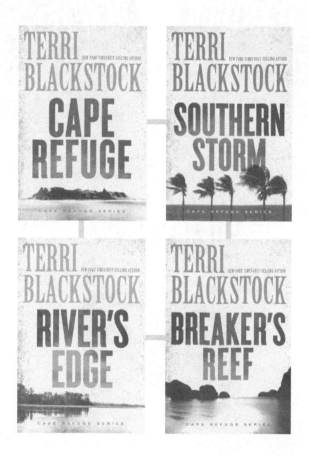

The Intervention Series

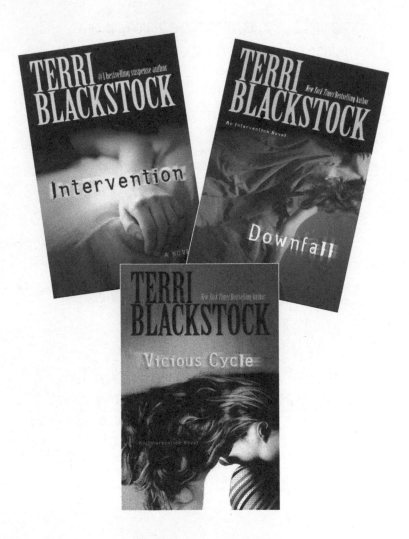

Available in print and e-book

Newpointe 911 Series

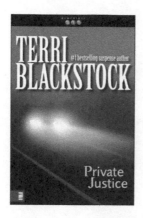

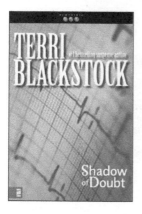

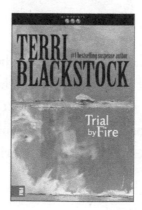

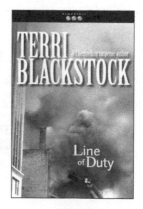

Available in print and e-book

ZONDERVAN®
.com

ABOUT THE AUTHOR

Photo by Deryll Stegall

Terri Blackstock has sold over seven million books worldwide and is a *New York Times* bestselling author. She is the award-winning author of *Intervention*, *Vicious Cycle*, and *Downfall*, as well as the Moonlighters, Cape Refuge, Newpointe 911, SunCoast Chronicles, and Restoration series.

www.terriblackstock.com
Facebook: tblackstock
Twitter: @terriblackstock